Chronicles of Bustos Domecq

BY JORGE LUIS BORGES
Ficciones
Labyrinths
Dreamtigers
Other Inquisitions 1937—1952
A Personal Anthology
The Book of Imaginary Beings
The Aleph and Other Stories 1933—1969
Doctor Brodie's Report
Selected Poems 1923—1967
A Universal History of Infamy
In Praise of Darkness
The Book of Sand

BY ADOLFO BIOY-CASARES
The Invention of Morel and Other Stories
Diary of the War of the Pig
A Plan for Escape

Chronicles of

JORGE LUIS BORGES

ADOLFO BIOY-CASARES

TRANSLATED BY
NORMAN THOMAS DI GIOVANNI

dep

A Dutton Paperback
E. P. DUTTON / NEW YORK

Sundry of these chronicles were warmly received and perspicaciously singled out for publication by the editors of the following—we frankly admit—outstanding periodicals (parenthetically are the titles under which these papers first appeared):

Antaeus: "In Search of the Absolute"

The Antioch Review: Foreword by Gervasio Montenegro, "The Selective Eye," "Naturalism Revived" (collected under the title "H. Bustos Domecq: Select Chronicles")

Encounter: "On Universal Theater" ("H. Bustos Domecq on Universal Theatre")

The New Yorker: "The Immortals," "An Evening with Ramón Bonavena"

The New York Times Book Review: "The Idlers" ("H. Bustos Domecq on Automation"), "The Flowering of an Art" ("H. Bustos Domecq on the New Architecture"), "An Abstract Art" ("H. Bustos Domecq on Gastronomy"), "A Brand-New Approach" ("H. Bustos Domecq on Revisionism")

The Scotsman: "Esse est Percipi"

Translation: "A List and Analysis of the Sundry Books of F. J. C. Loomis"

TriQuarterly: "Homage to César Paladión," "The Sartorial Revolution (I)," "The Sartorial Revolution (II)" (collected under the title "Three Chronicles of Bustos Domecq"), "The Brotherhood Movement" ("H. Bustos Domecq on the Brotherhood Movement")

This paperback edition first published in 1979 by E. P. Dutton, a Division of Elsevier-Dutton Publishing Co., Inc., New York

Assistance for the translation of this volume was given by the Ingram Merrill Foundation.

Published simultaneously in Canada by Clarke, Irwin & Company Limited, Toronto and Vancouver.

Library of Congress Cataloging in Publication Data

Bustos Domecq, Honorio, pseud.
  Chronicles of Bustos Domecq.
  Translation of Crónicas de Bustos Domecq.
  Includes index.
  I. Title.
PQ7797.B873C713   864   75-20182

ISBN: 0-525-47548-6
10 9 8 7 6 5 4 3 2 1

To those three forgotten greats—
Picasso, Joyce, Le Corbusier

Contents

Every absurdity has now a champion.
OLIVER GOLDSMITH (1764)

Every dream is a prophecy: every jest
is an earnest in the womb of Time.
FATHER KEEGAN (1904)

Foreword

Once again—this time upon the insistence of my old friend, the esteemed author—I front the inherent risks and pitfalls that so stubbornly strew the path of the writer of a preface. Not, however, that these escape the notice of my magnifying glass! We must steer a course, even as Odysseus himself, between two opposing reefs: Charybdis, *id est,* to spur the attention of the listless and somewhat careless reader with the fata morgana of attractions which the corpus of the tome will soon dispel; and Scylla, *id est,* to play down one's own brilliance so as not to overshadow and even nullify the pages that follow. The rules of the game are ineluctably laid down. Like the showy royal tiger of Bengal, which retracts its claws so as not to obliterate with a single swipe the features of its trembling tamer, we shall (without laying aside altogether the critical scalpel) obey the demands of the genre itself. In other words, we shall in these introductory remarks be faithful to truth, but even more so to Plato.

Such scruples, the reader will doubtless interpose, will prove illusory. Nobody would dream of comparing the sober elegance, the ability to hit the mark, the panoramic cosmovision of the present writer with the unsophisticated, unbuttoned, and somewhat casual prose of that truly good man who, in his spare time, dashed off—thick with dust and provincial tedium—these praiseworthy chronicles.

The rumor alone that an Athenian, a man of Buenos Aires (whose renowned name good taste forbids me to reveal), had consolidated the preliminary planning of a novel to be titled (unless I change my mind) *The Montenegros*—this rumor alone was enough that our beloved "Bugsy",[1] who once tried his own hand at narrative, should hasten, neither clumsily nor lazily, to criticism. We must admit that this brilliant step of shifting fields has yielded its reward. Discounting one or two inevitable blemishes, this little gathering of papers which it is now our privilege to preface shows quite a sufficiency of real value. That is to say, the book's contents provide the curious reader with an interest that its style alone would never nourish.

In the chaotic times in which we live, negative criticism is everywhere wanting in force, since its preponderant purpose is to uphold—beyond our pleasure or displeasure—national values, autochthonous values. These mark—here today, gone tomorrow—mere trendiness. In the present case, on the other hand, the preface to which I lend my signature has been obtained by the en-

[1] Affectionate nickname for H. Bustos Domecq used among his intimates. [Footnote by H. Bustos Domecq.]

treaty [2] of one of those friends to whom habit ties us. Let us, then, focus on achievements. From the vantage point granted him by his littoral Weimar, our secondhand shop [3] Goethe has engendered a truly encyclopedic compilation in which every feature of modernity finds its resonance. Whomsoever longs to dive into the depths of the novel, the lyric, the essay, conceptualism, architecture, sculpture, the theater, and the whole gamut of audiovisual media, which are so much the mark of our times, will, in spite of himself, have to come to terms with this indispensable vademecum, a true Ariadne's thread which will lead him by the hand all the way to the Minotaur.

A chorus of voices may well be raised denouncing the absence in this collection of some outstanding figure, who would blend in an elegant synthesis the skeptic and the sportsman, the high priest of letters and the stud, but this omission we attribute to the natural modesty of the book's author-craftsman, who knows his own limits, and not, more justifiably, to his envy.

On coolishly perusing the pages of this quite praiseworthy little opus, our drowsiness is for a moment shaken by a casual reference to one Lambkin Formento. An unexpected misgiving pangs us. Does such a personage, actualized in flesh and blood, exist? Is he not, perchance, a rela-

[2] This word is misemployed. Refresh your memory, don Montenegro. I asked you for nothing; it was you who turned up out of the blue at the printer's. [Footnote by H. Bustos Domecq.]

[3] After much explaining on the part of Dr. Montenegro, I insist no further and give up on the idea of sending him the registered telegram that I had Attorney Baralt draw up at my request. [Footnote by H. Bustos Domecq.]

tive, or at least an echo, of that Lambkin, the fictitious marionette, who gave his august name to one
of Hilaire Belloc's satires? This is the sort of thing
which tends to tarnish the potential carats of an
otherwise instructive repertoire and one that
aspires to no other endorsement—let us make this
perfectly clear—than that of probity, plain and
simple.

Equally unforgivable is the lightness with which
the author approaches the concept of
brotherhoodism when reviewing a certain baga-
telle in six overwhelming volumes poured forth
from the uncontainable keyboard of Attorney G.
A. Baralt. This plaything of the sirens of that legal
mind dwells overlong upon mere utopian combinations at the expense of true brotherhoodism,
which is a solid pillar of the present order and of
its most certain future.

In summary, what we have here is a little work
not altogether unworthy of our indulgent send-
off.

GERVASIO MONTENEGRO
Member, Argentine Academy of Letters

Buenos Aires, July 4, 1966

Chronicles of Bustos Domecq

Homage to César Paladión

To extol the manifold achievements of César Paladión, to wonder at the tireless hospitality of his mind, is—as we know—one of the truisms of contemporary criticism; yet, is it not worth bearing in mind that any truism, once in a while, yields a kernel of truth? The parallel to Goethe, then, is no less inevitable. It has often been suggested that the affinity between these two worthies is shown not only by their physical likeness but also by the more or less fortuitous circumstance that, in a way, they share an *Egmont*. Goethe declared that his whole spirit was open to the four winds; Paladión refrained from this affirmation (at least it is not included in his *Egmont*), but the thirteen protean volumes he has left us are proof that he might very well have adopted Goethe's dictum. Both men, Goethe and Paladión, exhibited that health and vigor which are the firmest foundation for the erection of the true work of genius. Hardy tillers in the fields of art, their hands guide the plow and mark out the perfect furrows!

The brush, chisel, shading stump, and modern camera have made Paladión's lineaments familiar the entire world over; still, those of us who knew him personally have undervalued—perhaps unjustly—so profuse an iconography. An iconography, it may be added, which does not always transmit the authority and the probity that the man radiated with a constant, gem-like, never-bedazzling-the-eye flame.

In the year 1909, César Paladión held the office of Consul of the Argentine Republic in Geneva, where he published his first book, *The Abandoned Parks*. The edition, which today is highly coveted among bibliophiles, was scrupulously corrected in proof by the author; but, nonetheless, the most outrageous misprints crept into the text, for, as it happened, its Calvinist typesetters were wholly innocent of the language of Sancho Panza. Those who thrive on gossip will be grateful for mention here of a rather regrettable episode which no one any longer remembers and whose single virtue was that it made abundantly clear the almost scandalous originality of the Paladionian theory of style. In the fall of 1910, a critic of considerable renown collated *The Abandoned Parks* with a work of the same title by the Uruguayan modernist Julio Herrera y Reissig, arriving—incredible as it may seem—at the conclusion that Paladión was guilty of plagiarism. Long extracts from both works, printed in parallel columns, justified, according to him, the daring indictment. The accusation, however, fell on deaf ears; not one reader paid it the slightest notice, nor did Paladión himself condescend to answer it. The muckraker, whose name I do not care to remember, comprehending his error soon enough, dropped into everlasting silence. His astounding critical blind spots lay fully exposed!

The period 1911–19 was one of almost superhuman fertility. From Paladión's pen, in rapid succession, came this outpouring: *The Pathfinder,* the pedagogical novel *Émile, Egmont,* and the *Eclectic Reader* (second series). At this point, under the pseudonym of H. Rider Haggard, he wrote the novel entitled *She,* using the Spanish version for young readers by Dr. Carlos Astrada (Buenos Aires, 1914).[4] Next came *The Hound of the Baskervilles, From the Appenines to the Andes, Uncle Tom's Cabin, The Province of Buenos Aires up until the Establishment of the Federal Capital, Fabiola, The Georgics* (in the Ochoa translation), and the *De divinatione* (in Latin). And then, in mid-career, death overtook him. From what inside information we have been able to garner, it appears that he had nearly completed the first draft of the *Gospel According to St. Luke,* a work of biblical character, of which unfortunately not a page has come down to us, but whose text would have been of the greatest interest.[5]

Paladión's methodology has been the subject of numerous critical monographs and doctoral theses, making any new discussion here superfluous. Let us concern ourselves, however, with a few

[4] It is perhaps worth noting that Paladión never again took up this particular pseudonym although his knowledge of the African scene was unerring, as may be evinced by even the slightest acquaintance with the book.

[5] On an impulse which reveals the man to the full, Paladión chose, as it seems, the standard version.

main points. The key has been given us, once and for all, in Farrel du Bosc's authoritative study *The Paladión-Pound-Eliot Line* (Paris: Viuda de Ch. Bouret, 1937). As du Bosc has stated definitively, quoting the words of literary critic Myriam Powell-Paul Fort, it is a case of "an amplification of units." Before and after Paladión, the literary unit that writers took from the common tradition was the word or, at most, the stock phrase. The long Byzantine centos, weaving together passages collected from various sources, were the earliest forerunners of the Paladionian technique; in our own time, a copious fragment from the *Odyssey* opens one of Pound's *Cantos,* and it is a well-known fact that the work of T. S. Eliot admits lines from Goldsmith, from Baudelaire, and from Verlaine. But Paladión, in 1909, had already gone further. He annexed, so to speak, a complete opus, Herrera y Reissig's *The Abandoned Parks.* A confidence leaked out by Maurice Abramowicz is one more proof of the delicate scruples and unswerving rigor that Paladión always brought to the arduous task of poetic creation: personally, he preferred *The Twilights of the Garden* by the Argentine poet Lugones, but he did not consider himself worthy of assimilating them; instead, he perceived that Herrera's book fell comfortably within his range at that time, inasmuch as in Herrera's pages he found a full expression of himself. Paladión granted the book his name and sent it on to the printer, neither adding nor omitting a single comma—a rule to which he remained ever after steadfast.

We are thus confronted by the major literary

event of the century—the appearance of Paladión's *The Abandoned Parks*. Certainly nothing could be further from the book by the same name by Herrera, which duplicated no earlier book. 1909! *Annus mirabilis!* At that moment, Paladión stood at the very threshold of his labors, of a life work such as no one before him had attempted. Reaching into the depths of his soul, he published a series of books that expressed him utterly— completely without overburdening the already unwieldy corpus of bibliography or falling into the all-too-easy vanity of writing a single new line. The unfading modesty of this man who, in spite of the lavish banquets tendered him by the well-stocked libraries of East and West, denies himself the *Divine Comedy* and the *Arabian Nights* and condescends, benevolent and smiling, to the *Eclectic Reader* (second series)!

The development of Paladión's mind has not been fully explained; for example, nobody as yet has interpreted that mysterious leap from the *Eclectic Reader* (etc.) to *The Hound of the Baskervilles*. For our part, we do not hesitate to put forward the theory that this course is not really out of the ordinary but follows the pattern of the writer of stature who, growing out of the romantic mold, crowns himself at last with all the noble serenity and limpid grace of classicism.

Let us make it clear that Paladión, aside from early schoolboy exercises, had no knowledge of the dead languages. In 1918, with a timidity that today touches our hearts, he published *The Georgics,* in the Spanish translation by Ochoa; a year later, by now aware of the range of his mind,

he sent the printer, in Latin, the *De divinatione*.
And what Latin it was! Cicero's!

Certain critics felt that to publish a gospel following the texts of Cicero and Vergil amounts to a kind of apotheosis of classical ideals; we prefer to see in this last step, which Paladión did not live to take, a spiritual renewal. In a word, the mysterious and clear path that leads from paganism to faith.

Everyone knows that Paladión had to pay out of his own pocket for the publication of his books, and that the small printings never exceeded the figure of three or four hundred copies. Today, of course, these books are virtually out of print, and the reader who is lucky enough to come upon a copy of *The Hound of the Baskervilles* and who is transported by so unmistakable a style, finds, in aspiring to relish *Uncle Tom's Cabin,* that this latter title is all but unavailable. For this reason we fully applaud the initiative of a group of congressmen, representing all parties, who propose a national authorized edition of the complete works of the most original and catholic of our men of letters.

An Evening
with Ramón Bonavena

All statistics, all work that is merely descriptive or
informative, imply the ambitious and perhaps
groundless hope that in the incalculable future
men like us, but with clearer minds, will infer
from the data that we leave them some useful conclusion or some hidden truth. Those familiar with
the six volumes of *North-Northeast*, by Ramón Bonavena, may, for all we know, suppose that further
elaboration is needed in order to crown and to
complement the body of work bequeathed by this
master. Let us, at the outset, give warning that the
foregoing remarks are the fruit of a personal reaction by no means authorized by Bonavena. The
only time I spoke with him, Bonavena flatly dis-
claimed the idea of any aesthetic or scientific significance in the work to which he had dedicated a
lifetime. That evening, after all the intervening
years, still stands out in my memory.

Along about 1936, I worked on the Sunday literary section of the *Evening News*. The editor, a
man whose far-ranging curiosity included, now

and then, the world of books, assigned me one typical Tuesday to interview the well-known but not yet famous novelist at his suburban retreat in Ezpeleta.

The house, which is still standing, was of one floor, though its flat roof boasted two rather small balconies in a pathetic hope of an upper story. Bonavena himself opened the door to me. The dark glasses, which make so brave a show in his better-known photos and which were part and parcel, it seems, of a passing ailment, did not that day adorn that face of vast and flabby jowls in which his features seemed to melt. After so many years, I believe I still remember his knee-length linen dustcoat and Turkish bedroom slippers.

His unforced politeness did not hide a core of reticence; at the outset, I attributed this to modesty, but soon it was evident to me that the man felt very sure of himself and awaited, without undue impatience, the hour of worldwide fame. Engaged in his pressing and almost endless task, he was grudging of his time, and the publicity I offered meant little or nothing to him.

In his study—that had about it something of the waiting room of a small-town dentist, with its pastel seascapes and its china figurines of shepherds and dogs—there were few books, and most of these were dictionaries of various disciplines and trades. The powerful magnifying glass and the carpenter's rule that I noticed on the green baize of his writing table did not surprise me in the least. Coffee and tobacco stimulated our conversation.

"Of course, I have read and reread your work,"

I said. "I believe, nonetheless, that in order to guide the common reader, the mass man, along a plane of relative comprehension, it would be helpful, perhaps, if you would sketch, in broad strokes and without going into great detail, the development of *North-Northeast* from the first seminal urge to the final vast production. I admonish—*ab ovo, ab ovo!*"

His face, until then gray and almost expressionless, brightened up. After a moment, his well-chosen words poured out in a torrent:

"My plan, at the beginning, did not exceed the bounds of literature, or, even worse, of realism. I wanted—there was nothing out of the ordinary about this, really—to produce a novel of the land, straightforward, with deeply human characters and the usual protest against absentee landowners. I thought of Ezpeleta, my own town. Indifferent to ivory-tower aesthetics, I meant to give open-minded testimony about a limited sector of local society. The first problems to come up were, perhaps, just trifles. The characters' names, for example. To call them by their real names might have exposed me to charges of libel. My lawyer, Attorney Ignacio B. Garmendia, whose office is just around the corner, assured me, as a bit of preventive medicine, that the average man of Ezpeleta is prone to litigation. I could always, of course, have invented names, but that might have opened the door to imagination. I opted for the use of initials, with asterisks—a solution that hardly satisfied me. Working my way into my subject, I came to realize that the major difficulty lay not in the characters' names but rather was of a psychological order. How was I to put myself into my neighbor's head? How was I to guess what others were thinking without abjuring realism? The answer was clear, but at first I could not see it. Then I considered the prospect of a novel in which the characters were domestic animals. But once again, how was I to intuit the cerebral processes of a dog, how was I to enter into a world perhaps less visual than olfactory? At a loss, I fell back on myself and thought that the one remaining possibility rested in autobiography. But even here lay the labyrinth. Who was I? Today's self, bewildered; yesterday's, forgotten; tomorrow's, unpredictable? What could be more unattainable than the mind? If I am self-conscious as I write, self-consciousness creeps in, a new factor; if I surrender to free association, I surrender to chance. I don't know whether you recall the story told, I believe by Cicero, of a woman who went to a temple to consult with an oracle and unaware of it spoke the very words of the answer she sought. Something similar happened to me here in Ezpeleta. Not so much in search of a solution but one day looking for something to do, I read over my notes. And there lay the key I was after. There, in the words *limited sector*. When I wrote them, I was simply using a commonplace; when I reread them, a sudden revelation dazzled me. *A limited sector* . . . What sector could be more limited than a corner of the deal table at which I worked? I decided then to restrict myself to one corner, to what that corner might offer. I measured with this carpenter's rule—which you may examine at your pleasure—the leg of the aforementioned table and

verified that it stood at thirty-one inches above
floor level, a height I deemed adequate. To have
gone on indefinitely upward would have meant to
knock my head against the ceiling, then the roof,
and quite soon astronomy; to have delved down
would have sunk me into the basement, out onto
the subtropical plain, if not into the very bowels of
the globe. The chosen corner, at least, offered no
lack of interesting possibilities. The copper ashtray, the blue-and-red pointed pencil, and so on,
et cetera."

At this point, I was unable to stifle my emotion,
and I broke in:

"I know, I know. You're talking about the second and third chapters, where we learn all about
the ashtray—the various shades of the copper, its
specific gravity, its diameter, the exact distances
and angles between the ashtray, the pencil, and
the edge of the table, and then the workmanship
of the twin china sheepdogs, and what they cost
wholesale and retail, and so many other facts no
less scrupulous than to the point. And as for the
pencil—an Eagle, an Eagle Chemi-Sealed No.
2B!—what can I say? You got it down so perfectly
and, thanks to your genius for compression, into
only twenty-nine pages—pages that leave nothing
to be desired by even the most insatiable appetite."

Bonavena did not blush. Without haste, without
pause, he again picked up the flow of dialogue.
"Ah, the seed has not fallen outside the furrow!
You are steeped in my work. As a bonus, I'll make
you this free gift of an oral appendix. One refers
not to the work itself but to the scruples of its creator. Once having exhausted the herculean labors

of recording the objects in their fixed places at the north-northeast corner of my writing table (an achievement that cost me two hundred and eleven pages), I asked myself whether it was legitimate to replenish the stock—*id est,* to introduce arbitrarily new articles, to deploy them within the magnetic field, and go on, without ado, to *describe them.* These objects, deliberately chosen for my descriptive tasks and brought from the far reaches of the room and even from the house, would never attain the casualness, the spontaneity, of the first series. Nevertheless, once located within the proper angles, they would become a part of reality and would demand the appropriate treatment. The marvelous grapple of the ethic and the aesthetic! This Gordian knot was cut by the sudden appearance of the baker's delivery boy, a most reliable young man, though a half-wit. Zanichelli, the half-wit in question, came to be, to use the common expression, my *deus ex machina.* His very density fitted him for the purpose. With trembling hope, almost as if committing an act of desecration, I ordered him to place something, anything, within the now vacant corner. He laid there a rubber eraser, a penholder, and, once again, the ashtray."

"The famous beta series!" I broke in. "Now I understand the enigmatic recurrence of the ashtray, which is repeated almost word for word, except for a few references to the penholder and eraser. More than one hasty critic thought he spotted a confusion—"

Bonavena stood up, towering. "In my work there are no confusions," he declared with justifiable gravity. "The references to the penholder and eraser should be a sufficient clue. With a reader like yourself, there's no point in detailing the later arrangements. Let it be enough to tell you that I shut my eyes, the half-wit placed one object or another, and then—hands to the task! In theory my book is infinite, in practice I claim my right to the rest I've earned—call it a halt by the wayside— after having evacuated page 941 of volume V.[6] At any rate, descriptionism is on the march. In Belgium there was recently celebrated the appearance of the first installment of *Goldfish Bowl,* a work wherein I have detected not a few heterodoxies. In Burma, in Brazil, in Boston, in Bayonne, active new centers are emerging."

Somehow, I felt that the interview was drawing to an end. I said, forestalling our goodbye, "Maestro, before I go I want to ask you one last favor. May I see some of the objects recorded in the book?"

"No," said Bonavena. "You will never see them. Each arrangement, before its substitution by the succeeding, was carefully photographed. In this way, I obtained a brilliant series of slides. Their destruction, on October 26, 1934, was most painful to me. More painful still was the destruction of the objects themselves."

I registered consternation. "What's that?" I managed to get out. "You brought yourself to destroy the black pawn of upsilon and the hammer handle of gamma?"

Bonavena looked at me sadly. "The sacrifice was

6 The whole world knows that a sixth volume appeared posthumously in 1939.

necessary," he explained. "The work, like the child who comes of age, must stand on its own feet. To have preserved the source material might have exposed it to irrelevant confrontations. Criticism might have fallen into the snare of judging it in terms of its more or less fidelity. In that way we would have lapsed into mere scientism. You are aware, of course, that I deny my work any scientific value."

Trying to console him, I said, "Of course, of course. *North-Northeast* is a work of art—"

"That's another mistake," pronounced Bonavena. "I deny my work any artistic value. It occupies, so to speak, a plane of its own. The emotions awakened by it, the tears, the acclaim, the grimaces, leave me quite indifferent. It has not been my intention to instruct, to uplift, to entertain, to gladden, or to move. My work is beyond that. It aspires to the humblest and highest of all aims—a place in the universe."

Firmly set on his shoulders, the solid head did not move. The eyes no longer saw me. I understood that the visit was over and left as best I could. *The rest is silence.*

In Search of the Absolute

It must be admitted, as much as it hurts, that the River Plate looks up to Europe and looks down on—or tends to ignore—authentic native values. The Nierenstein Souza case leaves no doubt as to this. Fernández Saldaña omits Nierenstein's name from the *Uruguayan Dictionary of Biography*. Monteiro Novato himself limits Nierenstein to his dates, 1879–1935, and to the bare listing of his best-known works: *The Panic Plain* (1899); *Afternoons of Amethyst* (1908); *Oeuvres et Théories chez Stuart Merrill* (1912), an intelligent study which earned the praises of more than one associate professor of Columbia University; *The Symbolism in Balzac's* La Rechèrche de l'Absolu (1914); and the ambitious historical novel *The Gomensoro Feud* (1919), which the author was to repudiate *in articulo mortis*. One searches Novato's haphazard notes in vain for the slightest mention of the Franco-Belgian literary dinners of fin de siècle Paris, which Nierenstein Souza attended, if only as a silent spectator, or for any mention of the posthumous miscellany *Bric-a-Brac,* published back in 1942 by a group of friends captained by yours truly, H. B. D. Nor does one find in Novato the least attempt to draw attention to Nierenstein's appreciable, though not always faithful, translations of Catulle Mendès, Ephraïm Mikhaël, Franz Werfel, and Humbert Wolfe.

Nierenstein's background, as is obvious, was broad. His native Yiddish had opened to him the gates of Teutonic literature; Father Planes had taught him Latin without tears; French he had suckled along with culture; and his English had been inherited from an uncle, who managed a British-owned meat-packing plant in Mercedes. Nierenstein guessed at Dutch and had a suspicion of the lingua franca of the Brazil-Uruguayan border.

With a second edition of *The Gomensoro Feud* in the press, Nierenstein retired to Fray Bentos, where, in the old family manor house rented him by the Medeiro family, he was at last able to dedicate himself fully to the painstaking composition of a masterpiece, the manuscript of which has become lost and whose very title is unknown. It was there, in that hot summer of 1935, that Atropos' scissors cut short the poet's stubborn stint and his almost monastic life.

Six years later, the editor of the *Evening News,* a man whose far-ranging curiosity now and then included the world of books, assigned me the task—somewhere between literary detection and piety—of tracing the remains of that magnum opus. The paper's cashier, after some natural reluctance, advanced me expense money for the voyage up the

Uruguay River—and it was certainly welcome. In Fray Bentos, the hospitality of a pharmacist friend, Doctor Zhivago, took care of the rest. This excursion, my first journey abroad, filled me—why not admit it?—with much-to-be-expected uneasiness. Although a study of the atlas failed to quell my anxiety, the assurances given me by a fellow-traveler that the natives of Uruguay have a solid command of our tongue did, finally, set my mind at rest.

I disembarked in the sister country one twenty-ninth of December. On the morning of the thirtieth, in the Hotel Capurro and accompanied by Zhivago, I put away my first Uruguayan café au lait. A notary entered into the conversation and—tossing off jokes right and left—he told us the story, not unknown back home among the jokesters of our beloved Corrientes Avenue, about the traveling salesman and the ewe. We went out into the blazing sun. No transportation proved necessary and, within a half hour, after admiring the town's exaggerated progress, we arrived at the poet's mansion.

Its owner, don Nicasio Medeiro, after handing around a quick liqueur and a few tidbits of cheese, debited us with the always new, always funny story of the old maid and the parrot. He assured us that the house—thank goodness—had been repaired by a part-time bricklayer but that the late Nierenstein's library was still intact owing to a temporary lack of funds for further improvements. In fact, there on shelves made of old orange crates we glimpsed an abundant series of volumes; on a work table we saw an inkpot over which a bust of

Balzac pondered; and on the walls were portraits of loved ones as well as an autographed photograph of George Moore. Donning my spectacles, I submitted the dusty volumes to an impartial examination. Here before me, predictably, were the yellow spines of the *Mercure de France,* which had had its day; the choicest works of Symbolist writing of the Nineties; a broken set of Burton's *Thousand and One Nights;* Queen Margaret's *Heptameron;* the *Decameron; Conde Lucanor; The Book of Calila and Dimna;* and the Grimms' *Fairy Tales.* Aesop's *Fables,* annotated in Nierenstein's own hand, did not escape my attention.

Medeiro allowed me to explore the drawers of the writing table. I spent two afternoons at the task. I shall say little of the manuscripts that I copied out, since Test Tube Editions, Inc., has just brought them before the reading public. The bucolic idyll of Punch and Judy, the tribulations of Moscarda, and the trials of Doctor Ox in search of the philosopher's stone are, by now, an indelible part of contemporary River Plate writing, despite the fact that some aristarch or other has spoken out against the preciousness of Nierenstein's style and the overall excess in his work of acrostics and digressions. Still, these little writings—no matter what virtues were found in them by the Uruguayan weekly *Marcha*'s most exacting critic— could not have been part of the magnum opus that our curiosity was ferreting out.

On the blank leaf at the end of one of Mallarmé's books, I came across this note by Nierenstein Souza: "How odd that Mallarmé, who was so intent on the absolute, should have sought it in

what is so uncertain and unstable—words. Everyone knows that their connotations change and that
even the most distinguished word stands in danger
of becoming trite or perishable tomorrow."

I also had a chance to copy out three successive
versions of one and the same alexandrine. In his
first draft, Nierenstein wrote:

To live for memory, forgetting almost all.

In *Breezes of Fray Bentos,* which was little more than
a house organ, the author preferred:

Things stored up by Memory for Forgetfulness.

The definitive text, which was to appear in the *Anthology of Six Latin-American Poets,* reads:

Memory lifts up its stores for Forgetfulness.

Another fruitful example is accorded us by this
pentameter line:

And only in the lost do we survive.

which became, in print:

Hang on encrusted in the flow of time.

Even the least attentive reader will note that in
both cases the published text is less graceful than
the draft version. The question intrigued me, but
some time was to pass before I got to the bottom
of the matter.

Somewhat disillusioned, I started off on my return journey. What would the bigwigs back at the *Evening News* say, having financed the trip? The clinging company of a certain fellow-passenger from Fray Bentos, whose name shall remain anonymous, did not contribute to the lifting of my spirits. This man shared my cabin and overwhelmed me with an endless litany of stories, for the most part unsavory and even shocking. I wanted to think about the Nierenstein case, but my insistent *causeur* refused to grant me the least truce. Along about daybreak I took refuge in the continued nodding of my head, an action somewhere between seasickness, sleepiness, and utter boredom.

Reactionary detractors of the modern subconscious will be reluctant to believe that on the gangplank of the South Docks Customs I hit upon the solution to the puzzle. I congratulated my nameless companion for his extraordinary memory and there and then I blurted out, "Where the devil did you get all these stories, my friend?"

His reply confirmed my sudden suspicion. He told me that Nierenstein had told him all, or nearly all, of them, and that Nicasio Medeiro, who had been a great intimate of the deceased, told him the rest. He added that the funny thing was that Nierenstein told stories very badly and that the locals actually improved them. All at once everything became clear—the poet's burning desire to attain the absolute in literature, his skeptical observation as to the impermanence of words, the progressive deterioration of his verses from one text to another, and the twofold personality of his library, which ranged from the hyper-refinements of the Symbolists to collections of purely narrative prose. Let us not be amazed by any of this. Nierenstein took up the tradition which, from Homer down to the hearth of the peasant cottage or to the gentleman's club, takes pleasure in inventing and listening to tales. The stories that Nierenstein made up he told badly, knowing that if they were worthy of it Time would polish them, as it has done with the *Odyssey* and the *Thousand and One Nights*. Like literature at its dawn, Nierenstein limited himself to the oral, not unaware that the years would end up writing it all.

Naturalism Revived

With great relief it comes to our notice that the descriptionism-descriptivism debate no longer makes headlines in the *Times Literary Supplement, The New York Times Book Review,* or other such bulletins. Nobody—not after the weighty lessons of Cyprian Cross, S. J.—can still be unaware that the former of the aforementioned terms finds its truest application in the area of the novel, whereas the latter is relegated to a whole gamut of items which includes, unquestionably, poetry, painting, and criticism. However, the confusion lives on and from time to time, to the scandal of all truth seekers, the name of Ramón Bonavena is linked with that of Hector Urbas. Perhaps to distract us from so great an absurdity, there is no end of those who perpetrate a second ridiculous coupling, that of Hilario Lambkin and César Paladión.

It is well to admit that such confusions are founded upon certain apparent parallels and terminological affinities; all in all, however, to the well-rounded reader a page of Bonavena will always be . . . a page of Bonavena, just as several pages of Urbas will always be . . . several pages of Urbas. Men of letters—all foreigners, to be sure—have propagated the nonsense of a descriptivist school here in the Argentine. On no other authority than that which in-depth talks with the luminaries of the would-be school confer on our modesty, we hereby affirm that this matter of descriptivism is not one of a structured movement or even less of Thursday-night literary dinners but is a phenomenon of the coming together of individuals.

Let us get to the bottom of the mystery. At the entrance of this exciting little descriptivist world, the first name that extends a hand to us (as you will have guessed) is that of Lambkin Formento.

Hilario Lambkin Formento's lot has been a rather odd one. The editors to whom he brought his work, which was generally very short and of little interest to the average reader, classed him as an objective critic—in other words, as a man who excluded from his comments all praise and all censure. His squibs, which many a time were but reproductions of the jackets of the books under review, began to incorporate details of their format, dimensions (in centimeters), weight, typography, quality of the ink, and porosity and scent of the paper. Between 1924 and 1929, without reaping either laurels or burrs, Lambkin Formento contributed to the back pages of *The Annals of Buenos Aires*. In November of the latter year, he gave up these duties in order to devote himself fully to a critical study of the *Divine Comedy*. Death overtook him seven years later, when he had already completed the three volumes which were to be, and are, the pedestal of his fame and which, respectively, are entitled *Inferno, Purgatorio,* and *Paradiso.* Neither the great public, nor even less his colleagues, understood what he had done. A cry of attention (to which the initials H. B. D. lent their prestige) was necessary for Buenos Aires, rubbing its sleepy eyes, to rise from its dogmatic sleep.

According to the immensely probable hypothesis of H. B. D., Lambkin Formento had, in a bookstall in Chacabuco Park, leafed through a copy of that white fly of seventeenth-century bibliography, *Travels of Praiseworthy Men,* whose fourth book informs us:

> . . . In that Empire, the craft of Cartography attained such Perfection that the Map of a Single province covered the space of an entire City, and the Map of the Empire itself an entire Province. In the course of Time, these Extensive maps were found somehow wanting, and so the College of Cartographers evolved a Map of the Empire that was of the same Scale as the Empire and that coincided with it point for point. Less attentive to the Study of Cartography, succeeding Generations came to judge a map of such Magnitude cumbersome, and, not without Irreverence, they abandoned it to the Rigors of sun and Rain. In the western Deserts, tattered Fragments of the Map are still to be found, Sheltering an occasional Beast or beggar; in the whole Nation, no other relic is left of the Discipline of Geography.[7]

[7] Quoted from Jorge Luis Borges' *A Universal History of Infamy,* p. 141, in the translation of Jorge Luis Borges and Norman Thomas di Giovanni; reprinted by joint permission of the translators and publisher. [Footnote by H. B. D.]

With his customary perspicacity, Lambkin re-marked among a circle of friends that a full-scale map presented great difficulties, but that an analo-gous method (or device) was not inapplicable in other fields—for example, literary criticism. To evolve a "map" of the *Divine Comedy* became, from that auspicious moment on, his life's aim. At first, he contented himself with publishing small, worn cuts of the plans of the circles of hell, the tower of purgatory, and the concentric heavens which adorn Dino Provenzal's distinguished edition of the work. Lambkin's exacting nature, however, would not be satisfied. The Dantesque epic still es-caped him! A second flash, which was soon after followed by a long, painstaking patience, pulled him out of his temporary marasmus. On February 23, 1931, it dawned on him that a description of the poem, in order to be perfect, had to coincide word for word with the poem in the same way that the famous map coincided point for point with the empire. After mature reflection, Lambkin did away with the introduction, notes, index, pub-lisher's name and address, and gave to the press Dante's work. Thus it was that the first monument of descriptivism was launched in our metropolis!

Seeing is believing: there was no dearth of book-worms who took, or pretended to take, this newest tour de force of criticism for just another edition of the well-known poem of Alighieri, using it as a copy of the text itself! Thus is the poetic muse falsely worshiped! Thus is criticism underestima-ted! Approval was unanimous and general when a hard-hitting decree of the Association of Booksel-lers (or, according to others, the Argentine Academy of Letters) prohibited this abusive use of the greatest exegetical endeavor in our midst within the city limits of Buenos Aires. The damage, however, had been done, confusion keeps snowballing, and there are scholars who stubbornly insist on likening such different products as Lambkin's analysis and the Christian eschatology of the great Florentine. There are even those who, bedazzled by the mere fata morgana of their similar systems of reproduction, link Lambkin's work with the diversified œuvre of César Paladión.

The case of Hector Urbas is somewhat different. This young poet, who today is reaching his fame, was almost a total unknown in September, 1938. His discovery is owed to those qualified men of letters of the outstanding jury who that year judged the Destiempo Publishers' poetry contest. The contest's theme, as everyone knows, was the classic, eternal subject of the rose. Pens and inkpots set themselves to the task; names of renown flocked; horticultural treatises, composed in alexandrines when not in iambic pentameter, were admired. Everything, however, paled next to the Columbus' egg of Urbas, who submitted, simple and triumphant—a rose. There was not a single dissident vote; words, those artificial daughters of man, were unable to compete with the spontaneous rose, daughter of God. Five hundred thousand pesos at once went to crown this unequivocal achievement.

Radio listeners, television spectators, even the rank amateur who now and then buys either the morning paper or those bulky world almanacs will by now, I am sure, have wondered at our delay in bringing up the case of Fernando Colombres. We make no bones, however, about suggesting that the obvious notoriety of such an episode—it was a typical darling of the yellow press—is owed less to its intrinsic value than to the timely intervention of the Municipal Ambulance Service and the emergency scalpel wielded by the golden hand of Dr. Gastambide. The event—who dares forget it?—is only too well remembered. Around that time (we are talking now of 1941), the Salon of Fine Arts had opened and special prizes had been arranged for works dealing with the Antarctic or Patagonian regions of the Argentine. We shall say nothing of the abstract or concrete interpretations of icebergs in stylized forms that led to the crowning of Winslow Hopkins' brow with laurel, but the main point here was actually Patagonian. Colombres, up till that time faithful to the most far-out extravagances of Italian neo-idealism, that year submitted a well-ventilated wooden crate which, on being opened by the authorities, let loose a bounding ram that quickly gored more than one member of the jury in the groin and, in spite of the horseman's agility with which he saved himself, injured painter-cattle breeder César Kirón's back. The ovine, far from being a more or less fictitious caricature, turned out to be an Australian-bred rambouillet Merino well endowed with a head of horns that left their stamp on the said respective zones of the injured. Like Urbas' rose, though in a more bruising and impetuous way, the aforementioned wool-bearer was not an artistic fancy but an actual, obstinate biological specimen.

For some reason that escapes us, the disabled

members of the jury denied Colombres the award that his artistic soul had looked forward to with appreciable hopes. The jury of the Rural Exposition showed itself fairer and more generous, however. These men were forthright in declaring our ram a champion, thanks to which, from that incident hence, it enjoyed the warmth and good wishes of the best Argentines everywhere.

The dilemma raised here is interesting. If the tendency to descriptivism continues, art runs the risk of sacrificing itself for the sake of Nature. The learned Thomas Browne long ago remarked that Nature was God's art.

A List and Analysis of the Sundry Books of F. J. C. Loomis

As regards the work of Federico Juan Carlos Loomis, it is comforting to realize that the era of slick jokes and of the facetiousness of incomprehension has long been relegated to oblivion. Neither does anyone any longer link Loomis' work to chance polemics with Leopoldo Lugones, around 1909, nor, later on, with the leaders of budding Ultraism. Nowadays, we are fortunate to be able to look on the master's poetry in all its naked fullness. It has been said that Gracián forecast Loomis' poetic achievement when he tossed out that famous phrase of his—no less perfect for being old hat—"What's good, if short, is twice as good," or, according to the teaching of don Julio Cejador y Frauca, "What's short, if short, is twice as short."

It is indubitable, moreover, that Loomis always disbelieved in the expressive power of the metaphor, which, in the first decade of our century, had been exalted by Lugones' *Lunario sentimental* and, in the Twenties, by such avant-garde reviews as *Prisma, Proa,* etc. We challenge even the cleverest critic to unearth—if we may be permitted an archeological term—a single metaphor in the entire range of Loomis' output, with the exception of those which stand exactly for their etymological meanings. We who preserve in memory, as if in a precious jewel case, those eloquent and copious all-night sessions at the author's home on Parera Street, sessions whose span embraced the two twilights, that of evening and that of the milky dawn, shall not easily forget the mocking diatribes of Loomis, the tireless *causeur,* against the metaphorists, who, to point the meaning of one thing, turn it into another. These diatribes, of course, owing to the very rigor of Loomis' work, never transcended the realm of oral expression. "Is not the evocation more alive and forceful in the word 'moon'," he would ask, "than in the image 'tea of nightingales', as Mayakovsky disguised it?"

More given to posing questions than listening to answers, Loomis would ask in the same vein whether a fragment of Sappho or one of those inexhaustible sentences of Heraclitus did not grow more and more through the ages than all the volumes of Trollope, the Goncourt brothers, and Tostado, which, in the face of memory, are obstinate.

One of the assiduous frequenters of our Parera Street Saturday nights was Gervasio Montenegro, who was no less charming as a gentleman than as the owner of a certain establishment out in the Chicago-like suburb of Avellaneda. Because of the multitudinous nature of Buenos Aires, where nobody knows anybody else, César Paladión, to the best of my knowledge, never *once* attended. How unforgettable it would have been hearing him hold forth, as an equal, with the master!

On one or two occasions, Loomis announced to us the immanent publication of a work of his in the hospitable pages of *Nosotros*. I recall the expectation with which we, his disciples, full of youth and enthusiasm, elbowed our way into Lajouane's bookshop in order to savor—first of the first—the *friandise* promised us by the master. Each time, however, our hopes were frustrated. Someone or other ventured a guess as to the use of a pseudonym (Evaristo Carriego's name aroused more than a single suspicion); somebody else imagined a malicious joke was afoot; somebody else again, a ruse to elude our genuine curiosity or to gain time; and there was even some Judas, whose name I wish not to recall, who suggested that Bianchi or Giusti, the editors of *Nosotros,* might have turned down the master's contribution. Loomis, a man of unimpeachable veracity, stuck to his story, repeating, with a smile, that his piece had been published without our having noticed. In our confusion, we even imagined that the magazine issued special numbers, which were withheld from the common herd of subscribers and the great mob, avid for knowledge, that infests libraries, bookshops, and newsstands.

Everything came clear in the autumn of 1911, when the windows of Moën's displayed the work later called *Opus 1*. And why not mention here and now the pertinent, straightforward title the author initially gave it—*Bear?*

At first, not many properly evaluated the painstaking labors that had preceded the writing of

Bear: the study of Buffon and Cuvier; frequent, attentive trips to our local zoo in Palermo; picturesque interviews with Piedmontese; the chilling and perhaps apocryphal descent into an Arizona cave, where a bear cub was sleeping its inviolable winter sleep; the acquisition of steel engravings, lithographs, photographs, and even of full-grown, stuffed specimens.

The preparation of his *Opus 2, Pallet,* carried Loomis to an unusual experiment, not without its hardships and risks—namely, a month and a half's roughing it in a slum dwelling on Gorriti Street, whose tenants, of course, never came to suspect the true identity of the polygraph, who, under the assumed name of Luc Durtain, shared their joys and sorrows.

Pallet, illustrated by the pencil of B.S., appeared in October, 1914. Deafened by the voice of distant cannon, the critics took no notice of it. The same happened to *Beret* (1916), a volume which suffers from a certain coldness, perhaps attributable to the demand it makes on the reader of having to learn French.

Scum (1922) is the least popular of the author's writings, in spite of the fact that the Encyclopedia Bompiani finds in it the culmination of what has come to be called the first Loomisian period. A temporary duodenal ailment suggested or imposed the subject of the above-cited work. According to the learned investigation of Farrel du Bosc, milk, the instinctive remedy of an ulcer patient, was the chaste and white muse of this modern Georgic.

The installation of a telescope on the roof of the

maid's quarters and the fervent, haphazard study of Flammarion's better known writings lay the groundwork of the second period. *Moon* (1924) marks the author's most poetical achievement, the open sesame that flung wide for him the great gates of Parnassus.

Then, the years of silence. No longer does Loomis frequent literary dinners; no longer is he the jovial master of ceremonies who, in the carpeted cellars of the Royal Keller, calls the tune. No more, no, does he leave his Parera Street residence. On the lonely roof the forgotten telescope rusts; night after night Flammarion's folios wait in vain. Cloistered in his library, Loomis turns the pages of Gregorovius' *History of Philosophies and Religions,* peppering its pages with queries and marginal notes and other jottings. We disciples later wanted to publish them, but this would have meant renouncing the teaching and the spirit of the glossarist. A pity, but what could be done about it?

In 1931, dysentery crowns what constipation had given rise to. Loomis, despite extreme physical distress, brings to a climax his masterwork, which was to be published posthumously and whose proofsheets we had the melancholy privilege of correcting. Is there anyone by now who can possibly be unaware that we allude to the famous volume which, either in resignation or in irony, is entitled *Perhaps*?

In the books of other authors, it must be admitted that there is a schism, a split between contents and title. The words *Uncle Tom's Cabin* do not readily communicate to us all the details of its plot.

To pronounce the words *Don Segundo Sombra* is not the same as having expressed each one of the horns, heads, hooves, flanks, tails, whips, saddle blankets, saddles, and shoeing aprons that, *in extenso,* make up the book. For Loomis, on the other hand, the title is the work. The reader marvels at the rigorous coincidence of both elements. The text of *Pallet,* for example, consists solely of the word "pallet." Story, epithet, metaphor, characters, suspense, rhythm, alliteration, social implications, the ivory tower, littérature engagée, realism, originality, the slavish imitation of the classics, syntax itself—all have been totally transcended. Loomis' life work, according to the malicious calculations of a certain critic less versed in literature than in arithmetic, consists of six words: "bear," "pallet," "beret," "scum," "moon," and "perhaps." This may be so, but behind these words what a wealth of experience, of vitality, of ripeness the artist has distilled!

Not everyone has known how to listen to the master's lesson. *Carpenter's Box,* the book of a would-be disciple, does no more than list—and like a chicken's flight, barely gets off the ground— chisels, hammers, saws, etc. Far more dangerous is the sect of the so-called "cabalists," who amalgamate the master's six words into a single puzzling phrase, fraught with perplexities and symbolism. Controversial, though well-meaning, seems to us the work of Eduardo L. Planes, the author of *Gloglocioro, Hröbfroga,* and *Qul.*

Eager publishers have long wanted to translate Loomis into various languages. The author, in spite of his pocket, rejected out of hand such

Carthaginian offers, which would have filled his coffers with gold. In these times of relativistic negativism, he upheld—the new Adam that he was—his faith in language, in simple and straightforward words that are at the reach of everyone. For Loomis, to write the word "beret" was enough to express that typical article of clothing with all its racial connotations.

To follow in the master's luminous wake is nigh impossible. If for a single moment, however, the gods were to grant us his eloquence and talent, we should obliterate all the preceding and limit ourselves to printing this sole and imperishable word—Loomis.

An Abstract Art

At the risk of wounding the noble sensibilities of all Argentines (whatever their particular or political persuasion), the fact must be faced that at this late date a tourist Mecca of the modern New World like Buenos Aires boasts but a single *tenebrarium*—located, at that, in a backwater of the city some several blocks from the nearest subway station. All things considered, however, the establishment stands for an effort worthy of the highest praise, for a real breakthrough in the Chinese wall of our general unfashionableness. More than one acute and far-ranging observer has dropped us the hint *ad nauseum* that the aforementioned *tenebrarium* is still far from holding its own with counterparts in Amsterdam or Basel or Paris or Denver, Colorado, or Bruges la Morte.

Without entangling ourselves in so ticklish a problem, we wish for the time being to pay homage to Ubalde Morpurgo, whose voice cries out in the wilderness from eight to eleven P.M. nightly except Mondays, backed—we must be frank—by a handful of cognoscenti who dutifully take turns at attendance. On two occasions, we ourselves have partaken of those symposia and, both times, save for Morpurgo himself, the half-glimpsed faces of the dinner crowd were never quite the same. Not so, of course, the contagious enthusiasm. Our memory shall never forget either the metallic music of the cutlery or the occasional crash of a breaking tumbler.

Delving into prehistory, it should be mentioned that this *petite histoire* began, like so many others— in Paris! The forerunner, as everyone knows, the beacon who got the ball rolling, was none other than the Flemish (or Dutch) Frans Praetorius. Long ago, Praetorius' lucky star drew him to a certain Symbolist café which was frequented, off and on, by the now justly forgotten Vielé-Griffin. Those were the good old days of the third or fourth of January, 1884! The ink-begrimed hands of the entire upcoming literary generation clamored over each issue of the magazine *Étape* as it came rolling hot off the press.

Let us go back in time to the Café Procope. Someone sporting a bohemian beret waves aloft an article buried at the back of the aforesaid publication; another, all petulance and military moustache, swears over and over again that he will not rest until he finds out who the author is; a third points with his meerschaum pipe to a person of timid smile and hairless head who, absorbed in his great blond beard, sits silent in a corner. Let light be shed on the mystery. The man upon whom astonished faces, pointing fingers, and gaping eyes focus is the Flemish (or Dutch) Frans Praetorius already alluded to.

The article is brief, and its dry-as-dust style smacks of test tube and alembic, but its authoritative tone soon musters a following. In its half page, not a single simile from Greco-Roman mythology is to be found, not a word is wasted. The writer sticks to his thesis—that the basic tastes are four: sour, salty, insipid, and bitter. This creed stirs discussion, provokes disagreement, but in the end for each unbeliever there are now a thousand devoted hearts. In 1891, Praetorius publishes the today classical *Les Saveurs;* let us not forget, by the way, that the Grand Man, yielding with unimpeachable good will to a host of unknown correspondents, adds to his previous catalogue a fifth taste, that of sweetness, which, for reasons it would be impertinent to go into here, had hitherto eluded his perspicacity.

Then, in 1892, an inveterate haunter of the Procope named Ishmael Querido throws open the portals of the almost legendary establishment Les Cinq Saveurs in a location just around the corner from the Panthéon des Invalides itself. The place is friendly and unassuming. For the payment of a small fee upon entrance, the eventual customer is entitled to one of five alternative choices: a lump of sugar, a cube of aloes, a cotton wafer, a grapefruit rind, or a *granum salis.* These items figure prominently in an early menu that it was recently our privilege to peruse in a certain *cabinet bibliographique* in the port city of Bordeaux.

In the beginning, to choose one of the five was

to deny yourself acquaintance with the other four, but in time Querido was to give the nod to succession, to rotation, and, finally, to mixing. He hardly reckoned, however, with the justified scruples of Praetorius, who argued that sugar besides being sweet tastes like sugar (who could refute this?) and that the admission of the grapefruit rind clearly constituted an infraction. It was a manufacturing pharmacist, the druggist Payot, who sliced the Gordian knot; he began furnishing Querido each week with twelve hundred identical pyramids, each an inch high and each affording the palate one of the now celebrated five tastes—sour, insipid, salty, sweet, and bitter. A veteran of these early campaigns has assured us that at first the pyramids were grayish and translucent and that later on, to make things easier, they were endowed with the five well-known colors, white, black, yellow, red, and blue.

Lured on, perhaps by the prospect of gain, perhaps by the word "bittersweet," Querido fell into the dangerous error of trying combinations. Even today purists accuse him of having pandered to public gluttony with his hundred and twenty pyramids of different shades of color. But such promiscuity led to Querido's rapid downfall; that selfsame year he was forced to sell his establishment to another chef, a nobody who desecrated the temple of tastes by selling, for Christmas purposes, stuffed turkeys. Praetorius commented philosophically, *"C'est la fin du monde."* [8]

[8] The French meaning is: " 'Tis the end of the world." [Joint note of the French Academy, the Argentine Academy of Letters, and the American Academy of Arts and Letters.]

In a certain sense this utterance was to prove prophetic to both forerunners. Querido, who spent his tottering years in the streets specializing in the sale of gumdrops, in the full summertide of 1904 finally paid his fare to Charon. Completely heartbroken, Praetorius managed to survive him by some fourteen years. The project of erecting a commemorative monument to each had the full backing of high government officials, the press, public opinion, the military-industrial complex, the turf club, the clergy, and the mostly highly reputed artistic and gastronomic circles. The funds allocated, however, did not permit the erection of two figures and so the sculptor's chisel had to limit itself to a single likeness that would synthesize the one's unkempt beard, the flat noses of the two, and the other's laconic stance. One hundred and twenty miniature pyramids worked in relief in the pedestal strike a note of freshness in the monument.

Both ideologists dispatched, we stand now before pure cookery's high priest, Pierre Moulonguet. His first manifesto dates from 1915; the *Manuel Raisonné* (three volumes in large octavo) from 1929. Moulonguet's theoretical tenets are so well known that we may safely limit ourselves here, God willing, to no more than the barest lifeless outline of them. The Abbot Brémond foresaw the possibilities of a poetry purely poetical; abstract and concrete artists—both words are obviously synonyms—strive after pictorial painting which condescends neither to anecdote nor to the slavish imitation of nature. In a like way, using weighty arguments, Pierre

Moulonguet plumped for what he daringly called "culinary cooking." Its aim, as the words imply, was a cuisine owing nothing to the plastic arts or to the object of nourishment. Vivid colors, elegant serving platters, and what common prejudice calls a well-presented dish—all these were banned; and banned was the crassly pragmatic orchestration of protein, vitamins, and the carbohydrates.

The age-old and ancestral tastes of veal, salmon, fish, pork, venison, mutton, parsley, *omelette surprise,* and tapioca—all dismissed by that cruel tyrant Praetorius—were now returned to astonished palates in the form (no compromising with the plastic arts) of a runny, grayish, mucilaginous mush. The diner, at last freed from the bonds of the much-touted five tastes, was again able to order himself fried chicken southern-style or coq au vin—but everything, as we know, took on the standard amorphous texture. Today as yesterday, tomorrow as today, and ever the same. A single nonconformist cast his shadow on the scene: we speak of Praetorius, who, like so many precursors, cannot tolerate the slightest deviation. He could not tolerate the slightest deviation from the path he had blazed thirty-three years earlier.

Victory, however, did not lack her Achilles' heel. A hand, any half-dozen fingers, are more than enough on which to count the now classic chefs—Dupont de Montpellier, Julio Cejador—unmatched in the art of turning the whole rich gamut of comestibles into the one runny mush demanded by the code.

But then in 1932 the miracle took place, worked by a cipher out of the crowd. Every reader knows his name: Jean-Françoise Darracq. J.-F.D. opened in Geneva a restaurant exactly like all others, serving dishes in no way different from those of the past: the mayonnaise was yellow, the greens green, the cassata a rainbow, the roast beef red. He was at the point of being dubbed a reactionary when then and there he laid the golden egg. One evening, in perfect calm, with a smile about to flicker across his lips and with that sureness of hand that genius alone commands, Darracq carried out the simple act destined to place him forever at the topmost point of the pinnacle in the entire annals of cookery. He snapped out the lights. There, in that instant, the first *tenebrarium* was launched.

The Brotherhood Movement

We should find it a pity were this essay, which aims mainly at eulogy and information, to distress the unprepared reader. Nonetheless, as the old Latin tag has it, *Magna est veritas et prevalebit.* Let us, then, harken [9] ourselves for the rude blow.

As the hackneyed story of the apple, whose plopping to the ground gave rise to the discovery of the law of gravity, is attributed to Isaac Newton, so is the story of misplaced footwear attributed to Attorney G. A. Baralt. The rumor runs that our hero, in great impatience to feast his ears on Moffo in *Traviata,* rigged himself up in such a hurry one night that he slipped his right foot into his left shoe and, vice versa, his left foot into his right shoe. This painful arrangement, while denying him full enjoyment of the overwhelming magic of both music and song, did reveal to him—in the very ambulance that removed him, finally,

[9] For "harken," read "hearten." [Author's note.] [10]

[10] For "hearten," we venture to suggest "harden." [Copy editor's note.]

from the topmost gallery of Buenos Aires' Teatro Colón—his now famous discovery of brotherhoods. Baralt, on putting his wrong foot forward, may have reflected that at any number of points on the globe, at that selfsame moment, other men and women were suffering an analogous mishap. In the popular imagination, it was this trifling accident that inspired him to his discovery.

The unvarnished truth, however, is that we personally got together with the attorney himself—capitalizing on a once-in-a-lifetime opportunity—in his now world-famous though cramped law office on Pasteur Street, in the heart of the Argentine capital, and that, always the gentleman, he dismissed the still popular fallacy out of hand, assuring us repeatedly that his theory of brotherhoods was the fruit of lengthy meditation upon the supposed laws of probability and the *ars combinatoria* of Raymond Lull, and that, as a matter of fact, in order to avoid catching bronchitis, he never ventured out of doors at night. So be it; gall is bitter, but undeniable.

The six tomes which Attorney Baralt saw into print under the overall title *Brotherhoods* (1947–54) make up an exhaustive introduction to the problem at hand. Together with the work of Ezra Fishpond and the Polish novel *Quo Vadis?*, by Ramón Novarro,[11] this six-volume set is found in any library worthy of the name, but it has been remarked that its mob of buyers is somewhat offset by a readership of zero. Despite its captivating

[11] For "Ramón Novarro," read "H. Sienkiewicz." [Copy editor's note.]

style, its copious indices and appendices, and the subject's irresistible glamor, the vast majority of bookbuyers has not been able to penetrate beyond the front endpapers and table of contents without losing their way like Dante in the *selva oscura.* To cite just one example, Cattaneo himself, in his prize-winning *Analysis,* progresses no farther than page nine of the "By Way of Preface," as he strays increasingly from the work itself to comment on a certain banned pornographic novelette by Bishop Cottone. For the foregoing reasons, we do not judge superfluous the present modest survey, which, though a pioneer effort, we hope will prove helpful in orienting the studious beginner. Our sources, what is more, are straight from the horse's mouth himself, since, rather than become embroiled in a perusal of the bulky work, we have found preferable conversational impact, in the flesh, with Baralt's brother-in-law Henri Gallach y Gasset, who, after a series of delays, resigned himself to admitting us into his now world-famous though cramped notary's office on Matheu Street, in the heart of the above-mentioned Argentine capital.

With quite remarkable rapidity, Gallach brought the brotherhood movement within grasp of our feeble reach. Humankind, he explained away, is made up, despite climatic and political differences, of a multitude of secret societies, or brotherhoods, whose members are not only unknown to each other but who may, at any given moment, change their status. Some of these societies are more enduring than others—for example, the society of individuals sporting Catalan surnames, or sur-

names that begin with the letter G. Others, in-
versely, quickly fade—the society of those who, at
this very moment, in Brazil or Africa, are inhaling
the odor of jasmine or, more culture-minded and
studious, reading a bus ticket. Other societies may
branch into subspecies which in themselves prove
interesting—for example, persons attacked by a
cigarette cough who, at the same time, may also be
wearing baggy trousers or be sprinting along on
ten-speed bicycles or be riding New York's Times
Square shuttle. Another sub-branch consists of
those individuals who hold themselves aloof from
the aforesaid—counting the nagging cough—only-
too-human characteristics.

Brotherhoodism, in short, is never at rest, but
flows like living sap. We ourselves, who do our
level best to maintain a position of blameless neu-
trality, just this evening belonged first to the fraternity of those riding the up elevator and, minutes later, to the fraternity of those riding
basementward or, claustrophobically, being stuck
somewhere between ladies' lingerie and home furnishings. The most trifling act—striking a match
or blowing it out—expels us from one group and
lodges us in another. Such widespread diversity
has a valuable discipline for character formation
built in: the person wielding a spoon is the adver-
sary of he who brandishes a fork, but very soon
both are at one over the use of the napkin, only to
split again over their Postum or Sanka. And all
without the slightest raising of the voice, without
the slightest gnashing of teeth—what harmony!
what an endless display of true integration! I think

you look like a turtle, and tomorrow I am taken for a tortoise, and so forth and so on!

There is no denying that so majestic a panorama opens itself, even if peripherally, to the blind stabs of certain self-appointed critics. As is always the case, the opposition sets in motion all sorts of contradictory objections. Channel 7 broadcasts that the whole scheme is old hat, that Baralt discovered nothing, since we have had, from time immemorial—we cite an American context—the A.F.L.-C.I.O., lunatic asylums, mutual aid societies, chess clubs, stamp albums, the Arlington National Cemetery, the Cosa Nostra, Congress, State Fairs, Botanical Gardens, the P.E.N. Club, drum majorettes, sporting goods stores, the Boy Scouts, bingo, and other groupings, which, no less useful for being well known, are a matter of common knowledge. The radio, on the other hand, bandies it about the airwaves that brotherhoodism, by the very flimsiness of the brotherhoods, is totally devoid of practical value. To one, the scheme is odd; to the other, old wine in new bottles. But the undeniable fact of the matter remains that brotherhoodism is the first planned attempt to unite on behalf of the individual all the latent affinities, which, up to now, like underground rivers, have coursed through history. Perfectly structured and steered by an expert helmsman, the brotherhood movement would constitute the bedrock of resistance against the lava-like torrent of anarchy. Let us, however, not shut our eyes to the inevitable offshoots of strife that the well-meaning doctrine may awaken: the man getting off a train will pull a switchblade on the man who boards; the incognizant buyer of gumdrops will try to strangle the master hand who dispenses them.

Equally aloof from detractors and adherents, Baralt marches his course. We are aware, from reliable sources (his brother-in-law himself!), that the good attorney has in progress a compilation of all possible brotherhoods. Of course, no lack of obstacles presents itself: let us only think, to take but one example, of the present brotherhood of persons who are thinking about labyrinths; of those who, a minute ago, forgot all about them; of those who two minutes ago forgot; of those who three minutes ago; of those who four minutes ago; of those four and a half; of those five. . . . Instead of labyrinths, let us take lamps. The plot thickens. Nor are cabbages and kings of any avail.

To end on a strong note, allow us to unburden ourselves of our warmest and weightiest approval. We have no idea how Baralt will steer clear of the reefs ahead of him; but we do know, with all the serene and mysterious certitude which faith alone can impart, that the Master will not fail to produce a catalogue that is all-embracing.

On Universal Theater

Nothing in this admittedly rainy fall season of 1965 is less up for debate than the fact that Melpomene and Thalia are the youngest Muses. After twenty-five or more centuries, the mask that wears the grin as well as the mask of her tearful sister have at last overcome (as drama critic Myriam Powell-Paul Fort has so often maintained) almost insuperable obstacles.

In the first place, there was the enslaving influence of names whose genius is above argument—Aeschylus, Aristophanes, Plautus, Shakespeare, Calderón, Corneille, Goldoni, Schiller, Ibsen, Shaw, Elmer Rice. In the second place, a succession of ingeniously wrought architectonic bulks that ranged all the way from those plain courtyards wide open to every rigor of drizzle and snow flurry (such as the one in which Hamlet delivered his monologue) down to the elaborate revolving stages of today's modern opera temples—to say nothing of such concomitant features as orchestra pits, prompters' boxes, and ladies' and gentlemen's powder rooms. In the third place, there were the overwhelming personalities of the mimes—Beerbohm Tree, that giant, etc.—who intruded between spectator and Art for no other purpose than that of reaping a rich harvest of applause. In the fourth and last place were cinema, theater of the air, and television, which, by purely mechanical means, broadened and popularized past evils.

Those who have unearthed the prehistory of the *new* New Theater wave aloft, as forerunners, two precursors: the Oberammergau Passion Play, performed by Bavarian farmhands; and those truly popular, multitudinous presentations of *William Tell*, which burgeoned out across cantons and lakes in the selfsame setting that first produced this (to be quite candid) hackneyed historical romance. Other investigators, even more antiquated, hark back to those guildsmen of the Middle Ages, who enacted the history of the world out of rustic oxcarts—fisherfolk performing Noah's Ark and contemporary pastrycooks the Last Supper. All this, though undeniably true, hardly blurs the now venerable name of Georg-Adolphe Bluntschli.

It was in the Swiss city of Ouchy, sometime back around 1909, that Bluntschli gained his much-discussed reputation as an eccentric. Time and time again, with a well-aimed jerk of his elbow, he tipped waiters' trays, managing to get himself soaked not infrequently in Kümmel when not in grated cheese. Typical—but apocryphal—is the incident on the grand staircase of the Gibbon Hotel of his having introduced his right arm into the left sleeve of a raincoat with a Scotch-plaid lining into which Baron Engelhart was struggling unsuccessfully to button himself up. Nobody would dream of denying, however, that he did put that swiftest of aristocrats to flight one day by the sudden display of an outdated Smith-Wesson made entirely of almond-studded chocolate. It has also been conclusively proved that Bluntschli was in the habit of venturing out onto the peaceful waters of Lake Geneva in a rowboat, where, under cover of darkness, he would mutter a brief aside or else allow himself a yawn. Further examples of his eccentricities are on record. We now definitely know that he smiled or sometimes sobbed in the funicular; and as to his conduct on streetcars, more than one witness has sworn as to having seen him swagger down the aisle, ticket tucked into the band of his boater, troubling some fellow passenger for the time. But around 1923, increasingly conscious of the significance of his Art, Bluntschli forswore such far-out experimenting. From this point on, he strolled along the streets, he found his way into offices and shops, he entrusted a picture postcard to a mailbox, he purchased tobacco and smoked it, he leafed through the morning papers, he behaved—in a word—exactly like the most inconspicuous of citizens.

Then, in 1925, he did what all of us end up doing (absit omen!)—he passed away one typical Thursday, well after ten P.M. Had it not been for the kindly-disposed disloyalty of his eternal friend, Maxime Petitpain, who in the unavoidable funeral harangue revealed it in words that are now classic, Bluntschli's message to the world would have been buried with him in the peaceful cemetery of Lausanne. Incredible as this may seem today, the address delivered by Petitpain and reproduced in its entirety in the biweekly *Petit Vaudois* had no repercussions whatever until 1932, when, from the back files of the newspaper, it was brought to light by the now celebrated actor and producer Maximilien Longuet. This promising young man, who had obtained the coveted Shortbread Award to study chess technique in Bolivia, ended by consigning to the flames—like Hernán Cortés before him—both chessmen and chessboard and, without as much as crossing the traditional Rubicon between Lausanne and Ouchy, gave himself up body and soul to those principles bequeathed posterity by Bluntschli.

In the back room of his bakery, Longuet brought together a limited but select group of illuminati who in their way not only constituted the posthumous executors of what has come to be called "the Bluntschli plan" but who also put this plan into action. Let us, in gilded capitals, stencil the names our memory still retains, even though they may be somewhat mixed up or even apocryphal—Jean Pees and Charles (or Charlotte) Saint Pe. This bold conventicle—on whose banner, we have no doubts, was inscribed the cry *"Out into the streets!"*—without an instant's delay confronted all the risks of public indifference. Not for a single second condescending to advertising gimmicks or to billboard posters, they went out, a hundred strong, into the Rue Beau Séjour. Not all of them left the aforesaid bakery at the same time. First, one threaded his quiet way due south, then another due northeast; a third rode on bicycle; not a few took the streetcar (some in patent-leather

74

boots). No one suspected a thing. The populous city took them for common passersby. The conspirators, showing exemplary discipline, neither greeted one another nor exchanged a wink. X strolled along the streets. Y found his way into offices and shops. Z entrusted a picture postcard to a mailbox. Charlotte (or Charles) purchased tobacco and smoked it. Tradition has it that Longuet waited at home, tense, biting his nails, his whole attention glued to the telephone, which at long last would bring him one of the two horns of the dilemma—*succès d'estime* or flat failure.

Is there any reader unaware of the outcome? Longuet, after the long centuries cited earlier, had struck a death blow to the theater of stage properties, set speeches, and box-office queues. The new theater stood on its own legs! The unprepared, the most ignorant, you yourself, are the actors; the script is life; and all the world's a stage.

The Flowering of an Art

Oddly enough, the term "functional architecture," which people in the profession hardly use anymore without a certain pious smile, has not lost its hold over the public at large. In hopes of clarifying the concept, the present essay shall, with a minimum of broad strokes, sketch a compact survey of the major architectural trends of the day.

The origins of the problem, though notably close to us, are blurred in polemical obfuscation. Two names compete for the roll of honor: Adam Quincey, who, in 1937, published in Edinburgh the strange monograph titled *Towards an Uncompromising Architecture;* and the Pisan, Alessandro Piranesi, who, barely a couple of years later, erected at his own cost the first Chaotic in history. (Unruly mobs, urged on by an insane itch to get inside the building, set it afire repeated times, to the point—one Halloween Night—of reducing it to a heap of tenuous ash. Piranesi was to pass away in the interim, but photographs and a plan have made possible the work of reconstruction, which, following more or less faithfully the general lines of the original, enables us once again to admire it.)

Reread in the cold light of present-day perspectives, Adam Quincey's short and badly printed study provides meager fare for those of us with a sweet tooth for novelties. Nevertheless, let us single out a page or two. In one passage, we read: "Emerson, whose memory was usually inventive, attributes to Goethe the concept of architecture as frozen music. That dictum and our own personal dissatisfaction with contemporary works have occasionally lifted us to the envisionment of an architecture that would, like music, be a direct language of the passions and not one subject to the demands of inhabitability." Further on, we read: "Le Corbusier speaks of the house as a machine for living—a definition which seems less applicable to the Taj Mahal than to an oak tree or to a fish." Such affirmations as these, obvious or platitudinous today, brought upon them at the time the fulminations of Gropius and of Wright, who were wounded in their innermost citadels, to say nothing of stirring a general uproar. The remainder of the monograph, torpedoing Ruskin's *Seven Lamps of Architecture,* now leaves us coldly apathetic.

It matters little or nothing whether or not Piranesi was aware of the aforesaid monograph. The undeniable fact is that he erected, on formerly malarial terrain along the Via Pestifera, with the help of masons and a volunteer corps of the elderly, the Great Chaotic of Rome. This noble edifice, which to some seemed a sphere, to others an ovoid, and to the reactionary a shapeless mass, and whose materials ran the gamut from marble to cow dung, consisted essentially of truncated bridges, of spiral stairways that gave access to impenetrable walls, of balconies to which entrance was impossible, and of doors that opened either into pits or into high, narrow rooms from whose ceilings soft armchairs and comfortable double beds hung upside down. Nor was there any lack of concave mirrors. In an initial burst of enthusiasm, *Architectural Forum* greeted it as the first concrete example of the new architectonic conscience. Who would have said then that the Chaotic, in a not too distant future, would be branded as half-hearted and outmoded!

We shall certainly not waste one drop of ink or one minute of time denouncing the coarse imitations that were opened to the public in the Disneylands of the Eternal City and in some of the leading fairgrounds of Paris.

Worthy of mention, though somewhat eclectic, is the sincretism of Otto Julius Manntoifel, whose shrine of the Many Muses, in Potsdam, brought together the revolving stage, the circulating library, the house as living unit, the winter garden, some flawless allegorical marbles, the Roman Catholic chapel, the Buddhist temple, the skating rink, frescoes, the polyphonic organ, the currency exchange, the men's room, the Turkish bath, and the wedding cake—to mention only a few of its elements. The burdensome maintenance of this multiple structure, however, caused it to be auctioned off and dismantled almost immediately following the festivities which crowned its opening. The date is significant: the twenty-third or twenty-fourth of April, 1941!

Now, inescapably, there looms before us a figure of even greater magnitude—the master of Utrecht, H. H. Verdussen. This peerless worthy not only wrote history but made it. In 1949, he issued a volume under the appropriate title *Organum Architecturae Recentis;* in 1952, under the patronage of Prince Bernhard, he opened to the public his House of Doors and Windows, to give it the affectionate name with which it was baptized by the entire population of Holland.

Let us summarize Verdussen's theory: walls, windows, doors, floor, and ceiling constitute beyond all discussion the basic elements of modern man's habitat. Neither the most frivolous countess in her boudoir nor the wretch in his death cell awaiting the stroke of midnight, which beckons him to the chair, can elude this iron law. It has come to us by rumor that a single hint from His Highness was enough to cause Verdussen to add two additional elements to his rigid plan—thresholds and stairways.

The building which carries out these principles covers a rectangular plot with a frontage of six yards and a depth of something slightly under eighteen. Each of the six doors that go to make up the façade of the ground floor, communicates, at a distance of some thirty-six inches, with a similar door, and so on in succession, until at the rear of the building we arrive at the eighteenth door. Severe paneling on each side divides the six parallel systems, which all together add up to the imposing sum of one hundred and eight doors. From the windows of houses across the street, the careful observer may make out that the second floor abounds in staircases of six steps that go up and down in zigzag form; that the third floor is made up entirely of windows; the fourth, of thresholds; and the fifth and last, of floors and ceilings. The building is of crystal, a characteristic which clearly facilitates examination from the outside. So perfect is this jewel, in fact, that no one has as yet dared copy it.

And so, having come down to the present, we conclude this brief sketch of the morphological evolution of Uninhabitable Dwellings, those concentrated refreshing whiffs of pure art which do not pander to the slightest trace of utilitarianism. Inside them, nobody finds his way, takes his ease, sinks himself down into comfortable funishings, greets the passerby from the inaccessible balcony, waves a handkerchief (or throws himself) from the upper windows. *Là tout n'est qu'ordre et beauté.*

P.S.: Galley proofs of the foregoing survey already corrected, word reaches us by cable from Tasmania itself of a new offshoot. Hotchkiss de Estephano, who until now had never overstepped the bounds of the most conservative circles of nonhabitable architecture, has launched a *J'accuse* that makes no bones about pulling the rug out from under the once respected Verdussen. The declaration argues that walls, floors, roofs, ceilings, skylights, doors, and windows—even if purely ornamental—are the bygone elements and fossils of a functional traditionalism which architects pretend to reject but which nonetheless still slip in by the back door. With widespread and dazzling publicity, he announces a new uninhabitable that does away with such relics while at the same time it avoids the all-too-easy expedient of mere bulk and shapelessness. With unflagging interest, we look forward to the models, plans, and photographs of this latest expression of the Modern.

Gradus ad Parnassum

Returning from a brief but not undeserved symposium on my work jointly sponsored by the universities of California (La Jolla) and Utah (Salt Lake City), what do I find awaiting me in one of the picturesque bars of our own Ezeiza International Airport but news of a decidedly funereal nature. It may safely be said that at a certain stage of life a man cannot turn around without someone dropping dead behind his back. In this case I refer, of course, to Santiago Ginsberg.

Here and now, I suppress the sadness occasioned by the loss of this bosom friend in order to rectify—if I may be allowed the word—the many erroneous interpretations of his work that have made their way into the daily press. I hasten to point out that in these flagrant absurdities I find no trace of malice; rather, let it be said that they are born of haste and pardonable ignorance. I shall set things straight, that is all.

Certain so-called critics seem to forget, more or less deliberately, that the first book published by

Ginsberg's pen was the poem-cycle entitled *Clues for You and Me*. My modest private library has in it, under lock and key, a copy of the first edition—*non bis in idem*—of this most interesting pamphlet. A sober jacket in a rich range of colors, a reconstruction of the author's face by Identikit, title by the publisher himself, typography by Bodoni & Co., text on the whole true to the manuscript—in plain fact, the book was a smash!

The date, A.D. July 30, 1923. The outcome was entirely predictable: a frontal attack by the Ultraists, the yawning neglect of the common herd of reviewers, one or two inconsequential notices, and, in conclusion, the prescribed dinner in the unpretentious Hotel Marconi on the near Westside. Nobody, it turned out, paid the slightest attention in the aforesaid sonnet sequence to certain blatant novelties that struck very deeply and that, every now and then, peeped through the work's humdrum triviality. I now single them out:

> In taproom chat the chums have gathered round
> While turnpike twilight falls without a sound.

Years later, K. Carter Wheelock was to be tripped up (*Treatise on the Adjective in the River Plate Region*, 1961) by the word "turnpike." The fact remains, however, that this word is to be found in any authorized edition—even in pocket form—of Funk & Wagnall's. Wheelock brands it "bold, felicitous, modern," and he puts forth the hypothesis—*horresco referens*—that the word is an epithet.

By way of example, this second flash:

The loving lips that kisses were to seal
While whispering, whispering, nocoameal.

I nobly confess that at first glance "nocoameal" here eluded me.

Let's try another sample:

Mailbox! The negligence of scattered stars
Denies the wise astrologer his wars.

For all we know, the opening word of this lovely couplet elicited not the least indictment from the critical brotherhood, an oversight justified perhaps by the fact that "mailbox," derived from the two words "mail" and "box," stands out conspicuously on page 204 of the sixteenth edition of the previously cited dictionary.[12]

In order to protect ourselves from entangling contingencies, we judged it precautionary, at the time, to register with the Copyright Office the formerly plausible hypothesis that the word "mailbox" was a mere slip of the pen and that the verse should read:

Hard knocks! The negligence of scattered stars

or, if you prefer:

Smallpox! The negligence of scattered stars . . .

May no one brand me traitor; I put my cards on the table. Sixty days after having registered the

[12] The identical words are also found, respectively, on pp. 509 and 100 of *Webster's New Collegiate Dictionary*. [Translator's note.]

above emendations, I dispatched a registered telegram to my good friend the author, explaining to him at length, without beating around the bush, the step I had taken. His reply baffled us. Ginsberg accepted our emendations on condition that the three variants under discussion should be taken as synonyms. What on earth could I do, I ask you, but bow my head? Clutching at straws, I took counsel with Frank Kermode, who gave the knotty problem his full attention, only to acknowledge that though every single one of the three hypotheses had its own undeniable attractiveness, no particular one gave him entire satisfaction. As may be seen, we were at a deadlock.

Ginsberg's second collection, subtitled *Bouquet of Perfumed Stars,* may be ferreted out in the basement of certain self-styled bookshops. The lengthy essay which the pages of the *New York Review of Books* dedicated to him, under the imposing signature of Jay Lee Parini, will for a long time remain definitive; but even so, as with so many other literary hands, the eminent Dartmouth professor failed to detect certain idiomatic anomalies which in their way make up the true·and weighty marrow of the volume in question. These anomalies take the form of words which are, generally speaking, so brief that they elude the critical magnifying glass: "drj," in the introductory quatrain; "ujb," in a now classic sonnet to be found in most school anthologies; "gnll," in the rondel "To His Beloved"; "hnz," in an epitaph bubbling over with restrained sorrow—but why labor the point? It is useless. We shall as yet say nothing of whole lines of which not a single word figures in Funk & Wagnall's!

Hloj ud ed pta jabuneh Jrof grugno.

The crux of all this would have remained in the air had it not been for the intervention of the undersigned, who furtively exhumed from an old built-in wardrobe-cum-bed a notebook (in Ginsberg's own hand), which the trumpets of fame will one of these days designate *Codex Primus et Ultimus*. Quite obviously it is a *totum revolutum* that lumps together sayings that captivated the mind of our amateur of letters ("The wheel that squeaks gets the oil," "To go from pillar to post," "Try and try again," et cetera, et cetera, et cetera), off-color doodles, signed essays, one hundred percent inspirational verses ("If—," by Rudyard Kipling; "How do I love thee? Let me count the ways," by Elizabeth Barrett Browning; "Paul Revere's Ride," by Henry Wadsworth Longfellow; "Say not the struggle nought availeth," by Arthur Hugh Clough), an incomplete selection of telephone numbers, and, not least, the most authoritative explanation of certain words, such as "turnpike," "gnll," "nocoameal," and "jabuneh," that figure in the Ginsberg canon.

Let us tread with caution. "Turnpike," which comes down to us (?) from "turn" and "pike," means, in the dictionary, "a toll road or one formerly maintained as such." Ginsberg is not in agreement with this. In his handwritten notebook, he suggests this: " 'Turnpike' in my verse denotes the emotion prompted by a melody that we have heard once, that we have forgotten, and that after some years we hear again."

Also, the veil is lifted on "nocoameal." Ginsberg specifically states: "Lovers repeat, without realizing it, that they have lived searching for each other, that they knew each other before ever meeting, and that their very happiness is the proof that they were always linked. To save time, to cut short such wordiness, I suggest that lovers simply say 'nocoameal' or, still more economical timewise, 'mapu' or, even better, 'pu.' " It is a great pity that the tyranny of metrics was to impose on Ginsberg the least euphonic of the three words.

Touching on "mailbox" in its locus classicus, I hold a great surprise for you. The word does not suggest, as the common reader might dream, the everyday artifact, cylindrical in shape and painted red, that assimilates letters through an orifice. On the contrary, the notebook instructs us that Ginsberg preferred the meaning "accidental, fortuitous, incompatible with a cosmos."

On this same train, without haste but without pause, the deceased resolves the greater part of the unknown quantities so worthy of the attention of the sloppy reader. Thus, to look into but a single example or two, we put forward that "jabuneh" means "the melancholy pilgrimage to places formerly shared with an unfaithful woman," and that "grugno," taken in its broadest sense, is equivalent to "letting out a sigh, an irrepressible plaint of love." We shall pass over the word "gnll" as over live coals; here the good taste that Ginsberg made his banner seems to have betrayed him.

Scruple compels us to copy out the following squib which, after so much tiresome explanation, leaves one exactly where we were in the first place:

> My aim is the creation of a poetic language, made up of terms which have no exact equivalent in common languages but which denote situations and sentiments that are, and always were, the essential theme of the lyric. The definitions that I have attempted with words like "jabuneh" and "mloj" are, the reader must remember, mere approximations. They are also a first effort. My followers will doubtless enrich my modest precursor's vocabulary. I ask of them that they not fall into purism; but, rather, let them alter, let them reshape.

The Selective Eye

The reverberation of a certain war of nerves, carried to a fever pitch by the A.A.A. (Association of Argentine Architects), that found its way into the yellow press and was spurred by the dark machinations of the technical director of the Plaza Garay, in the final analysis casts a crude, naked light on the postponed labors and much-respected personality of the most unbribable of our chisels, Antarctic A. Garay.

The whole affair brings back to memory, which is so prone to amnesia, heartwarming recollections of that unforgettable mackerel with French fries, washed down with a Rhine wine, that we savored in Freddy Loomis' dining chambers sometime around 1929. On that night, the most high-flown of the younger brood of the generation of that day—I speak of the literary side only—were gathered on Parera Street, lured there by the banqueting and by the Muses. The evening's final toast, drunk with champagne, was proposed by the gloved hand of Dr. Montenegro himself. Epigrams sparkled right and left, when not interspersed with ethnic gags. My nearest companion—seated at a corner of the table, where our waiter, that Tantalus in tails, overlooked our dessert—turned out to be a young man from the provinces, full of consideration and prudence, who never once batted an eye as I loftily held forth on the arts. On that occasion, at least, it must be admitted that my table companion kept up with my lengthy peroration. Later, as we were having ourselves a hot chocolate at an old grocery-bar àt the nearby Five Corners and close to the end of my analytical dithyramb on Lola Mora's fountain, Garay let me know that he was a sculptor. Sure enough, he proffered a printed announcement of an exhibition of his works being held for relatives and those with nothing to do at the salon of the Friends of Art, formerly the Van Riel. Before accepting, I left the bill up to him, payment of which he dawdled over for so long it ensured our missing the last streetcar and having to walk home.

For the opening, I put in a personal appearance. That first evening the show was steaming at full speed, sales dropping off only later to the point where not a single piece was sold. The stickers saying "Sold" fooled no one. As a matter of fact, the critics sugarcoated the pill as much as possible, alluding to Henry Moore and extolling the whole effort as praiseworthy. I myself, to repay the hot chocolates, penned an encomiastic line or two for the *Revue de l'Amerique latine,* taking cover, of course, behind the pseudonym "Foreshortened."

The exhibition did not break the old molds; it

was, in fact, made up of plaster molds, like those impressed on young minds in primary school by the drawing mistress, grouped in two and threes—acanthus leaves, feet, fruit. Antarctic A. Garay keyed us in to the fact that it was not the leaves or the feet or the fruit one was to regard but, rather, the space, or air, between the casts. This came to be what he called, according to my later explanation in the said publication in French, "concave sculpture."

The success of the first show was repeated in Number Two. This came to pass in a premises in the wholly typical neighborhood of Caballito. There was a single room without any other furnishings in sight than the four bare walls, a bit of molding here and there on the ceiling, and, on the planks of the floor, a half dozen pieces of rubble scattered at random. "All this," from the makeshift box office where I made a fortune hand over fist selling tickets at a quarter a head, I pontificated to the uninitiated, "really isn't worth a fig; the main thing, for those of sophisticated taste, is the space that circulates between the ceiling moldings and the rubble." The critics, who can't see beyond their nostrils, failed to grasp that an authentic development had taken place in the interim, and they only deplored the lack of leaves, fruit, and feet.

The results of this campaign, which without trepidation I declare unwise, were not long in making themselves felt. The public, jovial and good-natured at first, got fed up and, acting as one, set fire to the show on the very eve of the birthday of the artist, who suffered considerable contusions of the region vulgarly called the gluteus, owing to the impact thereupon of the chunks of rubble. As for the ticket-seller—yours truly—he got wind of what was coming and, so as not stir a wasp's nest, he packed up early, taking care to rescue the proceeds in a small cardboard suitcase.

My road was clear: I had to find a den, a nest, a hideout, where I could lay low when he of the contusions was released from the hospital. On the insistence of a Negro cook, I installed myself at the New Impartial, a hotel a block and a half from the Once, where I collected material for my detective study "Tadeo Limardo's Victim" [13] and where I never lost an opportunity to make a pass or two at Juana Musante, wife of one of the New Impartial's co-owners.

Some years later, in the Western Bar, having a hot chocolate and croissants, I was taken unawares by Antarctic A. Although recovered from his lesions, he had the tact not to bring up the subject of the little cardboard suitcase, and soon we resumed our inveterate friendship to the warmth of a second hot chocolate, which he once again paid for out of his own purse.

But why all this remembrance of the past when the present has taken over? I refer, as by now even the most obtuse reader must gather, to the stupendous show brought to a culmination in the Plaza Garay by the unrelenting labor and creative genius of our much-tried hero. Everything was planned sotto voce in the Western Bar. Beer stein alternat-

[13] N.B. We seize this opportunity to recommend to our buyers the immediate acquisition of *Six Problems for don Isidro Parodi*, by H. Bustos Domecq, soon to be available at better booksellers. [Footnote by H. B. D.]

ing with hot chocolate, the two of us, barely aware of what we consumed, conversed amicably. It was there and then that the artist whispered to me the preliminaries of his plan, which amounted to no more than a sheet-metal signboard bearing the notice "Sculptural Exhibition by Antarctic A. Garay." Once attached to a couple of two-by-fours, we were to plant it in a conspicuous place so as to be seen by anyone coming along Entre Ríos Avenue.

At first, I argued for Old English lettering, but in the end we settled for plain letters on a red background. With no municipal permission whatever and under cover of deepest night, while the watchman slept, we nailed up our sign in a rain that drenched both our heads. The deed committed, we dispersed in various directions in order to avoid being nabbed by the cops. My present domicile is just around the corner, on Pozos Street, but the artist had to hoof it all the way across town to the residential area of the Plaza de Flores.

The next day, slave of pure greed and to steal a march on my friend, I turned up with the rosy-fingered dawn at the green enclosure of the plaza as the first rays were lighting up the sign and the sparrows were chirping their good morning. A flat cap with an oil-cloth visor and a baker's dustcoat with mother-of-pearl buttons invested me with a look of authority. As for tickets, I had taken the precaution of keeping in my file the unused ones from the other time. What a difference between the humble—one might say casual—passersby, who paid their fifty cents without a grumble, and that mob of unionized architects who brought suit on us within three days! In spite of what the shysters allege, the matter is plain and simple. At the expense of much time and effort, our lawyer, Attorney Savigny, was persuaded of this at his now world-famous though cramped office on Pasteur Street. The judge, whom we might have to bribe with a small slice of the box-office takings should worse come to worse, now has the case under advisement. I am making ready, in advance, to have the last laugh. Everyone should know that Garay's sculptural œuvre, on show in the little plaza of the same name, consists of the space bounded by the buildings that line Solís and Pavón streets and reaching up to the sky itself, including, of course, the park's trees, its benches, its rill, and its perambulating citizenry. A selective eye—that is what's needed!

P.S.: Garay's projects keep growing apace. Indifferent to the outcome of the lawsuit, he is now dreaming up an exhibition (Number Four) which would take in the entire neighborhood of Núñez. Tomorrow—who can say?—his work, so exemplary and so Argentine, may come to incorporate the whole air space between the pyramids and the sphinx.

What's Missing Hurts Not

We once held that every age gives rise to its writer, its maximum organ, its true spokesman. The writer of our own accelerated times, as it happens, has taken up residence in Buenos Aires, where he was born on a certain twenty-fourth of August, 1942. His name—Tulio Herrera. His books— *Apologia* (1959); the poem collection *Rising Sooner* (1961), which took a Second Municipal Prize; and, in 1965, the completed novel *Let Light*.

Apologia owes its origin to an unusual episode, involving—so typical of our author—the plot woven by envy to impair the reputation of a member of his family, Father Ponderevo, six times accused of plagiarism. Relatives and outsiders alike could not help but recognize, in their heart of hearts, the steadfast devotion displayed by the young pen in his uncle's behalf. Not two years passed, however, before the critics were pointing out a rather singular feature of the work—the omission throughout of the name of the man being vindicated, as well as any reference whatever to the titles in question or to the dates of the works alleged to have served as the uncle's model. More than one literary bloodhound settled for the fact that these sleights of hand were owing to an extraordinary delicacy on the part of our author. Given the backwardness of the times, not even F. R. Leavis saw that we were dealing here with the first infiltration of a new aesthetic.

This selfsame aesthetic lent itself to development *in extenso* in the poetry of *Rising Sooner*. Drawn to the book by the apparent simplicity of its title, and buying a copy or two, the average reader did not examine—in the least—what was inside. He read the first line of verse

Ogre lives no roof at all

without suspecting that our Tulio had, like Icarus before him, taken drastic shortcuts. The golden chain was there still, but one or another missing link had to be reconstructed.

In certain—shall we call them concentric?—circles, the verse was branded obscure. What better way to shed light on it than by the following anecdote, made up from stem to stern, which gives us a glimpse of the poet on fashionable Alvear Avenue—dressed in a tight-fitting linen outfit, thin moustache, and spats—greeting the Baroness von Servus. As legend has it, he said, "Madame, how long since I've heard you bark!"

His meaning was obvious. The poet was referring to the Pekinese, which enhanced the lady. Apart from common courtesy, the little greeting reveals Herrera's doctrine in a single flash. Of the middle road nothing is said; we pass—O miracle of concision!—from the baroness to the barking.

This same methodology applies to the verse quoted above. A notebook in our possession and which we shall have printed the moment the still-active poet succumbs, cut off in the prime of youth and health, informs us that "Ogre lives no roof at all" was at the outset still more extensive. A number of amputations and loppings were necessary to bring out the synthesis which today we find dazzling. The early draft had a touch of the sonnet about it, and this is how it looked:

> Ogre of Crete, the Minotaur lives
> In a house of its own, the labyrinth.
> I, on the other hand, poor and unwell,
> Have no roof over my head at all.

As for the title, the words "rising sooner" constitute nothing less than a modern ellipsis of the age-old, dusted-off proverb—long since recorded by Correas in an embryonic stage—"Rising early brings dawn no sooner."

And now for the novel. Herrera, who sold us the four manuscript volumes of his draft, has for the time being forbidden us their publication, which is why we so look forward to the hour of his demise. Owing to the author's athletic makeup, however, this promises to be a dragged-out affair (Herrera being one of those who, when they take a deep breath, leave the rest of us panting for oxygen) and thus squelches any idea of that quick end which could satisfy the book-buying public's healthy curiosity. At any rate, having cleared it with legal counsel, we hasten to leak a summary of *Let Light* and its morphological evolution.

The title *Let Light* was, of course, taken straight from the Bible's "Let there be light: and there was light," omitting, as was inevitable, the words in between. The plot of the novel concerns the rivalry of two women, whose names are the same and both of whom are in love with the same man, who is mentioned in the book only once and even then by the wrong name, for the author tells us, in an outburst so typical of him (which, surely, does honor to him and to us), that his name was Rupert but that he called him Albert. It is true, certainly, that a Rupert is mentioned in chapter nine, but this is another Rupert and constitutes a clear case of homonymy.

The two women are engaged in a hard-fought competition, resolved by the administration of massive doses of cyanide in a spine-tingling scene that Herrera elaborated with the patience of an ant, and that, naturally, he left out. Another unforgettable cameo is provided by the moment the poisoner finds out—too late!— that she has exterminated her rival for nothing, since it was not with the victim but with the survivor that Robert was in love. This scene, which crowns the novel, had been planned by Herrera with an excessive array of details, but, so as not to have to leave it out, he never actually wrote it. What is above argument here is that this unexpected denouement, which we have had to sketch very superficially inasmuch as our contract quite literally muffles us, is perhaps the greatest achievement of the novel of today. The characters to whom the reader has access are simple supernumeraries, most likely drawn from other books, and have practically nothing to do with the plot. They linger in irrelevant conversation and are not even aware of what is taking place. Nobody suspects a thing, the reader least of all, and yet the work will be translated into several foreign languages and will obtain an honorable mention.

To be over and done, we promise in our capacity as executor the publication of the manuscript *in toto,* with all its lacunae and deletions. The work will be offered for sale by subscription, to be paid in advance, and will commence the moment the author expires.

At the same time, public subscription is still open for a bust to be erected over the author's common grave in the Argentine capital's Western Cemetery. The work will be by the sculptor Zanoni. In applying to it the example of the lamented polygraph, the sculpture will consist of an ear, a chin, and a pair of shoes.

The Multifaceted Vilaseco

Pens of the highest order—the crème de la crème of the Sexton Blakes of criticism—have flocked to spread the word that the manifold œuvre of Adalberto Vilaseco symbolizes, quite unlike any other, the development of Spanish-speaking poetry from the opening of this century down to our own day. Vilaseco's first turnout, the poem "The Soul's Burrs" (1901), born in an issue of the Fisherton (Rosario) *Overseas Courier,* is the engaging opusculum of the novice, still in search of himself, who crawls on all fours and, not infrequently, falls into sloppiness. The poem may be said to be more the work of a reader than a vigorous creator, since it is infested with influences, for the most part of others—namely, Argentina's own Guido Spano and Núñez de Arce, with marked leanings toward the Uruguayan folklorist Elías Regules. To sum all this up in a word, no one would any longer remember this youthful peccadillo were it not for the powerful light it sheds on Vilaseco's subsequent writings.

Several years later, our author published his "Melancholy of a Faun" (1909), whose length and meter were the same as those of his earlier composition. The new poem, however, was now marked with the seal of the modernism then in vogue. Next, Evaristo Carriego, the poet of the outskirts of Buenos Aires, was to have an impact on him, and it is from an issue of *Caras y Caretas* (dated November, 1911) that the third page we owe to Vilaseco comes down to us. This is the poem entitled "Masquerader." In spite of the extreme sway exercised over him by the singer of the fringes of the Northside of old-time Buenos Aires, there crops up in full force in "Masquerader" the unmistakable personality and lofty tone of the mature Vilaseco of "Kaleidoscope," the poem that materialized, above Longobardi's well-known vignette, in the review *Proa*.

Events do not come to rest there. The following year, Vilaseco was to turn out his willful satire "Viperine Lines," whose unusually severe language rid him—once and for all!—of a certain percentage of archaisms.

"Evita at the Helm" dates from 1947, and it was premiered with the greatest of fanfare in the Plaza de Mayo. Assistant Director of the Commission for Cultural Affairs only hours later, Vilaseco devoted his ensuing leisure to the projection of a poem which was to be—alas!—his last, for he passed away long before Tulio Herrera, who still clings to life for all he's worth.

"Ode to Integration" was Vilaseco's swan song, and it was dedicated to various statesmen. So it was that our poet's life was cut short in advanced old age, but not without his first having gathered in book form his uneven production. A touching private press edition, signed by the author *in articulo mortis* under our own friendly persuasion only moments before the undertaker bore him off, will make public his work among the select circle of bibliophiles who may wish to subscribe to the same by writing me at my home address on Pozos Street. Five hundred copies on featherweight paper, scrupulously numbered, more or less make up the *editio princeps,* which, upon receipt of cash payment, will be remitted by post, which these days is terribly unreliable.

Inasmuch as the book's exhaustive analytical preface, printed in fourteen-point italic type, was the responsibility of my pen, I was left materially impoverished, making for a certain diminution of spark in the analysis, which was why I was forced to appeal for a subsidy [14] to cover the costs of postage and handling. Instead of concentrating on the specific task at hand, the present factotum squandered precious time reading Vilaseco's seven lucubrations, So it was that I came to discover that, apart from their titles, the seven poems were exactly the same. Not a comma, not a semicolon, not a single word was different! This finding, the gratuitous fruit of chance, is, of course, of no importance to a thorough evaluation of the versatile Vilasiquian œuvre, and the fact that we mention it at all at this late date is only in the interests of sheer

[14] As to the identity of the subsidizer, consult the study "An Evening with Ramón Bonavena," included in the indispensable vademecum *Chronicles of Bustos Domecq* (New York, 1976), on sale at better booksellers.

curiosity. The *soi-disant* blemish adds to our edition an undeniable philosophical dimension, and it proves once more that, although minor details may bog down a pygmy, Art is one and unique.

Tafas, a Talented Brush

Swamped by the figurative wave in its vigorous backlash, the highly esteemed memory of an Argentine worthy, José Enrique Tafas, is endangered. On October 12, 1964, Tafas perished beneath the waters of the Atlantic at the fashionable seaside resort of Claromecó. Drowned young, mature only as a painter, he bequeaths us a rigorous doctrine and a resplendent body of work. It would be a deplorable mistake to confuse him with the faceless legion of abstract painters. Tafas, like them, arrived at an identical goal but by a quite different trajectory.

In my mind, in a preferential spot, I cherish the memory of a certain tender Septemberish morning when Tafas and I first met, courtesy of chance, at a newsstand that still displays its gallant profile at the south corner of Bernardo de Irigoyen Street and the Avenida de Mayo, in the very heart of the Argentine capital. Both of us full of the heady intoxication of youth, we had simultaneously appeared in person at the said emporium in search of the same Kodachrome postcard of the Café Tortoni. The coincidence proved decisive. Frank words crowned what smiles had already initiated. I shall not hide it that curiosity pricked me upon noticing that my new friend rounded out his acquisition with two additional postcards—one of Rodin's "Thinker" and another of the Hotel España.

Cultivators of art the pair of us, both inflated with trust, our conversation soon rose to the topics of the day. The circumstance that one of us was already a solid storyteller and the other an almost anonymous promise still lurking in a brush did not, as one might well have feared, spoil the talk between us. The tutelary name of Santiago Ginsberg, whose friendship we shared, served as our first bridgehead. The next thing, a critical anecdote of some relevant figure of the moment wormed its way into our conversation and, in the end, face to face over a steady flow of foaming steins—soaring, volatile talk on universal topics! We set a date to meet again for the following Sunday at The Mixed Train Tea Rooms.

It was on that occasion, after informing me of his distant Muslim origins (his father had come to these shores rolled in a rug), that Tafas tried to make clear to me what he was driving at with his easel. In the Koran, he explained, just as with the Jews of Junín Street, the painting of faces, of people, of features, of birds, of calves, and of other living beings is expressly forbidden. How was one to set brush and tube in motion without breaking Allah's commandment? After much trial and error, Tafas struck the right key.

A spokesman from the midland Province of

Córdoba had implanted it in Tafas that to be innovative in any art one has clearly to demonstrate that one has, so to speak, mastered it and can follow the rules like any old maestro. To break the traditional molds is the trend of our present age, but the would-be artist must first prove that he knows these molds like the palm of his own hand. As Lumbeira rightly pointed out, let us consume all we can of the tradition in advance of casting it before swine.

A truly wonderful person, Tafas took these sane words to his bosom and put them into practice in the following way: firstly, with photographic fidelity, he painted views of Buenos Aires (within a limited perimeter of the city) that copied hotels, cafés, newsstands, and statues. He never showed these pictures to anybody—not even to the inseparable friend with whom he shared many a stein of beer. Secondly, he erased them with bread dough and tap water. Thirdly, he gave them a coat of shoe blacking, so that his little paintings came out completely blackened. He was scrupulous enough, however, to label each one of his hodgepodges, which were now all the same—jet black—with its correct title, so that on each canvas you could read "Café Tortoni" or "Newsstand with Postcards."

The prices of these pictures, of course, were not uniform. They varied according to the chromatic details, the amount of foreshortening, the composition, etc., of the rubbed-out work. In the face of formal objections raised by groups of abstractionists, who refused to accept Tafas' titles, the Fine Arts Museum pulled off a real coup in acquiring three of the young master's eleven pictures. The sum paid was so astronomical that it left the taxpayer utterly speechless. Nonetheless, criticism in leading organs of public opinion leaned toward praise, but while A took a shine to one picture B took a shine to quite another—all, of course, within a climate of respect.

Such is Tafas' œuvre. He was, we have been informed, preparing a great mural with indigenous motifs, which he had in mind to record in the north and which once set down he would have submitted to the blacking process. What a great shame that death by water should have deprived us, the Argentine nation, of such a masterpiece!

The Sartorial Revolution (I)

According to the facts, the complex revolution began at the seaside resort of Necochea. The date, that interesting period that runs from 1923 to 1931; the leading actors, Eduardo S. Bradford and retired police chief Manuel M. Silveira.

Bradford, whose social background was rather dim, came to be an institution along the old wooden boardwalk, but that was no obstacle to his being seen as well at afternoon dancing parties, at charity fairs, at the celebration of children's birthdays, at silver wedding anniversaries, at eleven o'clock Mass, in the hotel billiards room, and in better summer homes along the shore. Many will recall the figure he cut: his soft Panama with its snap brim, his horn-rimmed glasses, his dyed handlebar moustache that did not quite hide the fine full lips, the wing collar and bow tie, the white suit with its set of imported buttons, the matching cuff links, the heeled boots that enhanced his middling stature—as all the while his right hand gripped a malacca cane and his left held a mouse-colored glove that softly flapped in the breeze off the South Atlantic.

His always amiable conversation circled the widest range of subjects, but invariably came back to the world of tailoring. Bradford was fond of pronouncing upon buttonholes, linings, shoulder padding, trouser cuffs, underclothes, haberdashery, velvet collars, scarves, spats, cream-colored garters, and—especially—winter apparel. Such a bias should not strike one as strange; Bradford was singularly sensitive to the cold, so much so that no one ever saw him bathe in the sea. Instead, he strolled the boardwalk from end to end, his head sunk down into his shoulders, arms crossed or hands in his pockets, and his whole frame shaking with the shivers.

Another idiosyncrasy that did not elude the eye of the keen observer was that, in spite of the watch chain connecting his lapel to his left pocket, he mischievously refused to give anyone the time. Also, though his liberality was beyond a doubt, he never picked up a check, nor was he ever known to press the smallest coin upon a beggar. On the other hand, he was often nagged by a cough. Sociable as could be, he nonetheless maintained—with praiseworthy aloofness—a discreet space between himself and others. His favorite motto: *Noli me tangere.* He was friendly to everyone but opened his door to no one, and up until that fated third of February, 1931, the cream of Necochea never suspected his actual place of residence. One of the witnesses testified that a few days earlier he had seen Bradford enter Quiroz' paint shop with a billfold in his right hand, and come out again with the same billfold plus a heavy cylindrical package.

No one, perhaps, might ever have rung down the curtain on his guise had it not been for the perspicacity of retired chief Silveira, a man who had won his stripes dealing with the Cosa Nostra in Rosario, and who, spurred on by a bloodhound instinct, came to have his suspicions.

Over the course of several seasons, Silveira tracked Bradford with every caution, although Bradford—who seemed quite unaware—night after night gave Silveira the slip, thanks to the darkness on the outskirts of Necochea. The activity of the tireless sleuth was the talk of the town, and consequently many a citizen gave Bradford the cold shoulder, their cordiality passing from a former hearty give-and-take to a dry nod of the head. However, accredited families rallied round him and with a nobility of sentiment expressed their loyalty. That was not all; on the boardwalk certain newcomers appeared who followed in Bradford's footsteps and who, under close examination, were dressed in an identical way, though in paler shades and with a frankly down-and-out aspect about them.

The bomb hatched by Silveira did not take long to go off. On the above-mentioned date, two plainclothesmen, headed up by the chief himself, appeared in person at the door of a small wooden shack on one of those still unnamed streets far out beyond the town limits. They knocked and called out repeated times, then finally forced the door and, revolvers in hand, broke their way into the rickety dwelling. Bradford surrendered on the spot. He raised his hands, but did not let go of his malacca cane nor did he take off his hat. Without losing a moment, the policemen threw a sheet around him that had been brought along expressly for that purpose, and off they whisked him while he sobbed and trembled. His scanty weight drew their attention.

Accused by the prosecuting attorney, Leonidas Codovilla, of breach of trust and indecent exposure, Bradford immediately gave in, thereby letting down his backers. Truth prevailed, self-evident. From 1923 to 1931, Bradford, the gentleman on the boardwalk, had strolled the town of Necochea naked. Hat, horn-rimmed glasses, moustache, collar, necktie, watch chain, suit and set of buttons, malacca cane, gloves, handkerchief, and heeled boots were but drawings, in color, applied to the *tabula rasa* of his epidermis. In such a hopeless predicament, the timely influence of strategically placed friends might have rescued him, but unfortunately a circumstance came to light that totally estranged him from everyone. His financial position left much to be desired! It seemed he had not even the wherewithal to scrape together enough to get himself a pair of eyeglasses. He had been forced to paint them on, in the very way he painted on everything else— including the malacca cane. The judge brought down on the accused the full penalty of the law. After the trial, Bradford, in the martyrdom of the State Penitentiary, revealed himself as the pioneer he was. He died there of bronchial pneumonia, wearing no more than a striped suit stubbornly drawn on his lean flesh.

In the wake of all this, Carlos Anglada (with that nose of his for smelling out the most remunerative aspects of modern life) dedicated a series of articles to Bradford in *Vogue*. President of the

Commission Pro-Bradford's Statue on the ex-Wooden Boardwalk of Necochea, Anglada got together a considerable number of signatures and contributions. As far as we know, nothing concrete has come of the monument.

More cautious and highminded, perhaps, was don Gervasio Montenegro, who gave a short course at summer school on pictorial wardrobes and the eventual unrest this might create among members of the needle trades. But Montenegro's hairsplitting and reluctance to commit himself were quick to give rise to Anglada's now famous plaint—"Even after death they slander him!" Not satisfied with this alone, however, Anglada challenged Montenegro to put on the gloves in a ring of his choice, but, too impatient to wait for the reply, Anglada was last seen boarding a jet for Boulogne-sur-Mer. Meanwhile, the sect of the Picts had multiplied its ranks. The latest and boldest of them fronted the inherent risks and began imitating the Pioneer and Martyr down to the last T. Others, by nature inclined to the *pian piano,* resorted to a middle road: a real toupee, but a painted monocle or an indelibly tattooed suit coat. About their trousers we choose to preserve silence.

But such precautions were useless. The reaction had set in! The Honorable Kuno Fingerman, who at the time was head of the Public Relations Office of the Center for Woolen Products, published a volume entitled *The Aim of Clothing Is to Keep Oneself Warm,* which he soon after followed up with a sequel called *Let's Bundle Up!* Such shots in the dark found their echo in a group of young men who, driven by a quite understandable urge for positive action, came rolling out into the streets, spherically wrapped in something they named Total Suits, which—devoid of a single opening—completely enclosed their happy owners from head to foot. The most highly favored materials for the Total Suit were tanned hides and waterproof canvas; a later refinement, intended to deaden the knocks, was the wraparound woolen mattress.

Nevertheless, the aesthetic touch was missing. This was supplied by the Baroness von Servus, who launched a new departure. As a first measure, she went back to verticalism and to the freedom of the arms and legs. In connection with a mixed group of metalworkers, artists in crystal, and makers of lamps and lampshades, she constructed what came to be known as Plastic Attire. Except for the problem of its weight—which no one has as yet denied—this attire allows the wearer all the mobility desired. Consisting of metal plates or sections, and reminiscent of the deep-sea diver and the medieval knight, Plastic Attire is highpointed by a show of revolving flashing lights that are designed (and guaranteed) to bedazzle the passerby. It also sends out intermittent tintinnabulations that many class as useful and melodious as automobile klaxons.

Two rival trends evolved from the Baroness von Servus, who (according to hearsay) gives her blessing to the second. The first is the somewhat dandified Downtown Look; the other, of a more popular flavor, is Uptown Casual. Partisans of both followings agree, despite bitter antagonism, on keeping themselves in the main indoors and out of sight.

The Sartorial Revolution (II)

If, as has been duly pointed out, the epithet *functional* is wholly out of fashion in the small world of architects, in sartorial circles it has attained prestigious and dizzying heights. Clearly, men's clothing presented a rather vulnerable flank to the onslaught of younger generations. On the part of the hidebound there has been a signal failure to justify the beauty—or even the utility—of lapels, trouser cuffs, buttons that do not button, the knotted tie, and the hat band (or, as the poet has it, the "frieze of the fedora"). And so the scandalous arbitrariness of such useless embellishments has finally come under the public eye. In this respect, Poblet's [15] condemnation is unanswerable.

It may be worthy of note that the new order springs from a passage by the Anglo-Saxon Samuel Butler. Butler remarked that the so-called human body is a material projection of the mind and that, when you come down to it, there is

[15] J. D. F. Poblet (or Pobblet), b. 1894. [Translator's note.]

117

hardly any difference whatever between the microscope and the eye, inasmuch as the former is merely an improvement on the latter. The same, according to the trite riddle of the sphinx, might be said of the walking stick and the leg. The human body, in brief, is a machine: the hand no less than the Winchester, the buttocks than a wooden (or electric) chair, the skater than the skate. This is why the itch to flee from machinery is meaningless; man is but a working sketch to be supplemented, finally, by horn-rimmed glasses, by crutches, and by the wheelchair.

As is not infrequent these days, the great leap forward was born of the happy coupling of the dreamer (who operates in the dark) and the business tycoon. The former, Professor Lucius Scaevola, was responsible for the general theory; the latter, the tycoon, was practical-minded Pablo Notaris, owner of the popular Red Monkey Hardware & Kitchenwares, Inc., now refurbished from basement to roof and universally known as Scaevola-Notaris Functional Tailoring, Ltd. We cordially invite the reader to pay a visit, without cost or obligation, to the modern establishment of the aforementioned firm of Messrs. Scaevola and Notaris, where he will be warmly welcomed and will receive the utmost in personal attention. A well-trained staff is on hand to see to the full satisfaction of the reader's every need, providing him—all at low, low prices—with the patented All-Round Glove, whose two components (matching, down to the last detail, the hands of the buyer) include every single one of the following finger extensions: *On the right hand*—The Thumb Drill, The

Index Corkscrew, The Middle-Finger Fountain-pen, The Ring-Finger Rubber Stamp, The Small-Finger Penknife; *on the left hand*—The Thumb Awl, The Index Hammer, The Middle-Finger Skeleton Key, The Ring-Finger Umbrella-Walk-ingstick, and finally, the Small-Finger Scissors. (No substitutions, please.) Other customers, perhaps, may wish to be shown the All-Purpose Highhat (second floor), which permits the easy conveyance of food products and valuables, to say nothing of a variety of things better left unmentioned. Not yet in stock but coming soon is the File-Suit, whose leading feature is the replacement of the old-fashioned pocket with the sliding drawer. The Trouser-Seat with built-in Double Steel Springs—at first opposed by the chairmaker trades—has so won the general approval of the buying public that its overwhelming success leaves us at liberty to omit it from this pre-paid advertisement. Remember, readers, shop now and save later!

A Brand-New Approach

Paradoxically, the notion that happened to carry the day at the World Congress of Historians recently held at Pau, in the south of France—the concept of a pure history—is exactly what constitutes the major obstacle to the full understanding of the said congress. In open contravention of this very thesis, we have entombed ourselves in the basement of the Argentine National Library, Periodical Division, consulting a variety of the same from July of this year. The multilingual bulletin which recorded verbatim the bristling debates and the conclusion that was arrived at is in our hands. The principal theme of the congress was "Is History a Science or an Art?" Observers noted that the contending sides held aloft, each claiming for its own camp, the same names—Thucydides, Voltaire, Gibbon, and Michelet. (We shall not let pass here the pleasant opportunity of congratulating the delegate from our northern province of the Chaco, Mr. Gaiferos, who gallantly proposed to the other members of the congress that they give a preferential place to our own Indo-America, beginning, of course, with the Chaco, that obvious seat of more than a single worthy.) The unforeseen, as it so often does, came to pass. The thesis that aroused the unanimous vote turned out to be, as is now well-known, the one put forward by Luigi Zevasco that History is an act of faith.

Truly the propitious hour was ripe for the congress to give its consensus to this proposal which, sudden and revolutionary on the face of it, had already been prepared after much rumination by the long patience of the centuries. Actually, there is no handbook of history, even down to schoolboy textbooks, that has not long since anticipated, more or less offhandedly, some precedent or other. The dual nationality of Christopher Columbus, for example; the victory of Jutland, which, in 1916, was attributed to Saxon and Hun alike; the seven birthplaces of Homer, a writer of note—these are only a handful of cases that spring to the mind of the average reader. In all these instances there beats, embryonic, an unquenchable will to affirm what is one's own, the indigenous, the *pro domo*. At this very moment, as with an open mind I turn out this discerning chronicle, our eardrum is deafened by the controversy raging over tango king Carlos Gardel—darling of Buenos Aires to some, an Uruguayan to a few, when in point of fact he hailed from Toulouse. How akin this is to the controversy over the stamping ground of the old-time outlaw Juan Moreyra, now so hotly disputed by the progressive towns of Morón and Navarro. I but mention the business about Leguisamo, who, I am afraid, is hopelessly Uruguayan.

Let us return to Zevasco's pronouncement:

"History is an act of faith. Archives, records, archeology, statistics, hermeneutics, the facts themselves matter little. History's commitment is to history—freed of all trepidation and scruples. Let the numismatist put away his coins and the papyrologist his papyruses. History is a blast of energy, is a life-giving breath. Exalter of power, the historian exaggerates, he inebriates, he emboldens, he encourages. No tampering, no softening, our watchword is to reject out of hand that which does not build strength, that which does not positivize, that which is not glory."

The seed sprouted. Thus the destruction of Rome by Carthage is a paid holiday observed since 1962 in the region of Tunis; thus the annexation of Spain to the tethered nomadism of the imperialistic Querandí Indian is, nowadays, here in the Argentine, a truth backed by a fine.

The versatile Poblet, like so many others, has once and for all settled it that the exact sciences not be based on the accumulation of statistics. In order to teach the young that three plus four make seven, you do not add four cakes plus three cakes nor four bishops plus three bishops nor four cooperatives plus three cooperatives nor four patent leather buttons with three wool socks. Once the principle has been intuited, the youthful mathematician grasps that three plus four invariably make seven and he does not have to prove it over and over again with chocolates, man-eating tigers, oysters, or telescopes. The same methodology is required of history. Does a military defeat suit a nation of patriots? Certainly not. In the latest textbooks, approved by the respective authorities, Waterloo is to France a victory over the hordes of England and Prussia; so too is Appomattox, all over the American south, a stunning victory.

At the outset, some coward or other held that such revisionism would break down the unity of the discipline of history and, what is worse, would put out on a limb the publishers of world histories. At present, we have reason to believe that this fear is truly groundless, since even the most nearsighted person must understand that the proliferation of contradictory statements rises from a common source, nationalism, and confirms *urbi et orbi* Zevasco's dictum. Pure history brims, to a considerable extent, with the honest revenge of each nation. Mexico has thus recovered, in print, the oilwells of Texas, and we here in the Argentine, without risking the skin of a single native son, have recovered the south polar cap and its inalienable archipelago.

There is more. Neither archeology nor hermeneutics nor numismatics nor statistics are, in this day and age, ancillaries. They have at long last regained their independence and, equated with History—their mother—they have become pure sciences.

Esse est Percipi

As an old roamer of the neighborhood of Núñez and thereabouts, I could not help noticing that the monumental River Plate Stadium no longer stood in its customary place. In consternation, I spoke about this to my friend Dr. Gervasio Montenegro, the full-fledged member of the Argentine Academy of Letters, and in him I found the motor that put me on the track. At the time, his pen was compiling a sort of *Historical Survey of Argentine Journalism*, a truly noteworthy work at which his secretary was quite busy, and the routine research had accidentally led Montenegro to sniff out the crux of the matter. Shortly before nodding off, he sent me to a mutual friend, Tulio Savastano, president of the Abasto Juniors Soccer Club, to whose headquarters, situated in the Adamant Building on Corrientes Avenue near Pasteur Street, I hied.

This high-ranking executive still managed to keep fit and active despite the regimen of double dieting prescribed by his physician and neighbor, Dr. Narbondo. A bit inflated by the latest victory of his team over the Canary Island All-Stars, Savastano expatiated at length between, one maté and another, and he confided to me substantial details with reference to the question on the carpet. In spite of the fact that I kept reminding Savastano that we had, in yesteryear, been boyhood chums from around Agüero and the corner of Humahuaco, the grandeur of his office awed me and, trying to break the ice, I congratulated him on the negotiation of the game's final goal, which, notwithstanding Zarlenga and Parodi's pressing attack, center-half Renovales booted in thanks to that historic pass of Musante's.

In acknowledgment of my support of the Abasto eleven, the great man gave his maté a posthumous slurp and said philosophically, like someone dreaming aloud, "And to think it was me who invented those names."

"Aliases?" I asked, mournful. "Musante's name isn't Musante? Renovales isn't Renovales? Limardo isn't the real name of the idol acclaimed by the fans?"

Savastano's answer made my limbs go limp. "What? You still believe in fans and idols?" he said. "Where have you been living, don Domecq?"

At that moment, a uniformed office boy came in, looking like a fireman, and he whispered to Savastano that Ron Ferrabás wished a word with him.

"Ron Ferrabás, the mellow-voiced sportscaster?" I exclaimed. "The sparkplug of Profumo Soap's after-dinner hour? Will these eyes of mine see him in person? Is it true that his name is Ferrabás?"

"Let him wait," ordered Mr. Savastano.

"Let him wait? Wouldn't it be better if I sacri-

ficed myself and left?" I pleaded with heartfelt ab-
negation.

"Don't you dare," answered Savastano. "Arturo,
tell Ferrabás to come in."

What an entrance Ferrabás made—so natural! I
was going to offer him my armchair, but Arturo,
the fireman, dissuaded me with one of those little
glances that are like a mass of polar air.

The voice of the president began deliberating.
"Ferrabás, I've spoken to De Filippo and Ca-
margo. In the next match Abasto is beaten by two
to one. It's a tough game but bear this in mind—
don't fall back on that pass from Musante to Renovales. The fans know it by heart. I want imagination—imagination, understand? You may leave
now."

I screwed up my courage to venture a question.
"Am I to deduce that the score has been
prearranged?"

Savastano literally tumbled me to the dust.
"There's no score, no teams, no matches," he said.
"The stadiums have long since been condemned
and are falling to pieces. Nowadays everything is
staged on the television and radio. The bogus ex-
citement of the sportscaster—hasn't it ever made
you suspect that everything is humbug? The last
time a soccer match was played in Buenos Aires
was on June 24, 1937. From that exact moment,
soccer, along with the whole gamut of sports,
belongs to the genre of the drama, performed by a
single man in a booth or by actors in jerseys before
the TV cameras."

"Sir, who invented the thing?" I made bold to
ask.

"Nobody knows. You may as well ask who first

thought of the inauguration of schools or the showy visits of crowned heads. These things don't exist outside the recording studios and newspaper offices. Rest assured, Domecq, mass publicity is the trademark of modern times."

"And what about the conquest of space?" I groaned.

"It's not a local program, it's a Yankee-Soviet co-production. A praiseworthy advance, let's not deny it, of the spectacle of science."

"Mr. President, you're scaring me," I mumbled, without regard to hierarchy. "Do you mean to tell me that out there in the world nothing is happening?"

"Very little," he answered with his English phlegm. "What I don't understand is your fear. Mankind is at home, sitting back with ease, attentive to the screen or the sportscaster, if not the yellow press. What more do you want, Domecq? It's the great march of time, the rising tide of progress."

"And if the bubble bursts?" I barely managed to utter.

"It won't," he said, reassuringly.

"Just in case, I'll be silent as the tomb," I promised. "I swear it by my personal loyalty—to the team, to you, to Limardo, to Renovales."

"Say whatever you like, nobody would believe you."

The telephone rang. The president picked up the receiver and, finding his other hand free, he waved it, indicating the door.

The Idlers

The nuclear age, the curtain-drop on colonialism, the rise of the military-industrial complex, the challenge of the left, the zoom in the cost of living and concomitant shrinking of the pay envelope, the Papal call to peace, the threat of the devaluation of the dollar, the spread of sit-down strikes, the proliferation of supermarkets, the conquest of space, the population shift from rural life to city slums, the passing of rubber checks—all these spell quite an alarming panorama and, when you come right down to it, give the man of the Sixties food for thought. But the diagnosis of evils is one thing, the remedy another. Without wishing to venture in prophecy, we nonetheless make bold to suggest that the recent importation of Idlers into the Argentine Republic with a view to their ultimate manufacture here, may—in acting as a form of sedative—greatly contribute to the lessening of tensions so widespread in the nation today. The supremacy of the machine is a fact no one any longer disputes; the Idler, it turns out, is but one more step in this inevitable process.

Which, one may ask, was the first telegraph, which the first tractor, which the first Singer sewing machine? Questions such as these nonplus the intellectual mind. With respect to Idlers, however, no such problem exists. No iconoclast the world over would dream of denying that the original Idler first revved its intricate motors in Mulhouse, and that its undisputed begetter was the engineer Walter Eisengardt (1914–41). Two distinct personalities were at conflict in that notable Teuton— one, that of the incorrigible dreamer, who published an estimable yet utterly forgotten monograph on that thinker of the yellow race, Lao Tse; the other, the solid and down-to-earth man of action with practical bent of mind, who, after designing any amount of purely industrial machinery, on June 3, 1939, gave birth to the first recorded Idler. We are speaking of the model now on display at the Mulhouse Museum. Barely over four feet long, two feet high, and eighteen inches wide, it nontheless contained nearly every last one of its eventual basic elements—all the way from its metal tanks to its glass conduits.

As is the case in any border town, one of the inventor's maternal grandmothers sprang from Gallic stock, and, in the upper circles of her neighborhood, went by the name of Germaine Baculard. The pamphlet that serves as the main source of the present painstaking study states flatly that that elegance peculiar to Eisengardt's work comes from his sprinkling of Cartesian blood. We entirely uphold this charming hypothesis, which, it may be added, enjoys the approval of Jean-Christophe Baculard himself, the Great Alsatian's successor and publicizer. Eisengardt, killed in a Bugatti motorcar accident, did not live to see the spate of Idlers now rampant in factories and office buildings throughout the world. (God grant him power from heaven to view them, reduced to specks by the intervening distance and—for that very reason—closer to the prototype he personally hand-designed!)

Now for a thumbnail sketch of the Idler, slanted to those readers who have heretofore shirked their duty of paying a visit to San Justo (only twenty-seven miles southwest of Buenos Aires on Route 3) to inspect the specimen on display there at the Ubalde Piston Works. The monumental artifact, filling the breadth of the terrace at the heart of the factory yard, reminds us after a fashion of an out-sized linotype. Twice the height of U. P. W.'s chief foreman, its weight is said to be computed in several sand tons. Not only is it made of iron, but its color is that of iron painted black.

A stepped gangplank allows the conscientious tourist to scrutinize and touch it. At the same time, if he puts his ear to the majestic contraption, from the machine's innards he can make out a slight throbbing and may even detect distant rumblings. In effect, the Idler hides in its interior a system of conduits through which water and an occasional crystal globe run in the darkness.

Nobody in his right mind would fall into the error of believing that the Idler's physical frame-work is of greater importance than the mood it casts over the masses of humanity who swarm around it. On the contrary, what counts most about the Idler is the awareness it creates that in its bowels, secret and silent, beats something that plays and sleeps.

The goal envisioned during Eisengardt's romantic wide-awake nights is now wholly attained. Wherever an Idler is found, the machine rests, and man, reinvigorated, works on.

The Immortals

And see, no longer blinded by our eyes.
RUPERT BROOKE

Whoever could have foreseen, way back in that innocent summer of 1923, that the novelette *The
Chosen One* by Camilo N. Huergo, presented to me
by the author with his personal inscription on the
flyleaf (which I had the decorum to tear out before offering the volume for sale to successive men
of the book trade), hid under the thin varnish of
fiction a prophetic truth. Huergo's photograph, in
an oval frame, adorns the cover. Each time I look
at it, I have the impression that the snapshot is
about to cough, a victim of that lung disease which
nipped in the bud a promising career. Tuberculo-
sis, in short, denied him the happiness of acknowl-
edging the letter I wrote him in one of my characteristic outbursts of generosity.

The epigraph prefixed to this thoughtful essay
has been taken from the aforementioned novelette; I requested Dr. Montenegro, of the Academy, to render it into Spanish, but the results were
negative. To give the unprepared reader the gist
of the matter, I shall now sketch, in condensed

form, an outline of Huergo's narrative, as follows:

The storyteller pays a visit, far to the south in Chubut, to the English rancher don Guillermo Blake, who devotes his energies not only to the breeding of sheep but also to the ramblings of the world-famous Plato and to the latest and more freakish experiments in the field of surgical medicine. On the basis of his reading, don Guillermo concludes that the five senses obstruct or deform the apprehension of reality and that, could we free ourselves of them, we would see the world as it is—endless and timeless. He comes to think that the eternal models of things lie in the depths of the soul and that the organs of perception with which the Creator has endowed us are, *grosso modo*, hindrances. They are no better than dark spectacles that blind us to what exists outside, diverting our attention at the same time from the splendor we carry within us.

Blake begets a son by one of the farm girls so that the boy may one day become acquainted with reality. To anesthetize him for life, to make him blind and deaf and dumb, to emancipate him from the senses of smell and taste, were the father's first concerns. He took, in the same way, all possible measures to make the chosen one unaware of his own body. As to the rest, this was arranged with contrivances designed to take over respiration, circulation, nourishment, digestion, and elimination. It was a pity that the boy, fully liberated, was cut off from all human contact.

Owing to the press of practical matters, the narrator goes away. After ten years, he returns. Don Guillermo has died; his son goes on living after his fashion, with natural breathing, heart regular, in a dusty shack cluttered with mechanical devices. The narrator, about to leave for good, drops a cigarette butt that sets fire to the shack and he never quite knows whether this act was done on purpose or by pure chance. So ends Huergo's story, strange enough for its time but now, of course, more than outstripped by the rockets and astronauts of our men of science.

Having dashed off this disinterested compendium of the tale of a now dead and forgotten author—from whom I have nothing to gain—I steer back to the heart of the matter. Memory restores to me a Saturday morning in 1964 when I had an appointment with the eminent gerontologist Dr. Raúl Narbondo. The sad truth is that we young bloods of yesteryear are getting on; the thick mop begins to thin, one or another ear stops up, the wrinkles collect grime, molars grow hollow, a cough takes root, the backbone hunches up, the foot trips on a pebble, and, to put it plainly, the paterfamilias falters and withers. There was no doubt about it, the moment had come to see Dr. Narbondo for a general checkup, particularly considering the fact that he specialized in the replacement of malfunctioning organs.

Sick at heart because that afternoon the Palermo Juniors and the Spanish Sports were playing a return match and maybe I could not occupy my place in the front row to bolster my team, I betook myself to the clinic on Corrientes Avenue near Pasteur. The clinic, as its fame betrays, occupies the fifteenth floor of the Adamant Building. I went up by elevator (manufactured by the Electra

Company). Eye to eye with Narbondo's brass shingle, I pressed the bell, and at long last, taking my courage in both hands, I slipped through the partly open door and entered into the waiting room proper. There, alone with the latest issues of the *Ladies' Companion* and *Jumbo,* I whiled away the passing hours until a cuckoo clock struck twelve and sent me leaping from my armchair. At once, I asked myself, What happened? Planning my every move now like a sleuth, I took a step or two toward the next room, peeped in, ready, admittedly, to fly the coop at the slightest sound. From the streets far below came the noise of horns and traffic, the cry of a newspaper hawker, the squeal of brakes sparing some pedestrian, but, all around me, a reign of silence. I crossed a kind of laboratory, or pharmaceutical back room, furnished with instruments and flasks of all sorts. Stimulated by the aim of reaching the men's room, I pushed open a door at the far end of the lab.

Inside, I saw something that my eyes did not understand. The small enclosure was circular, painted white, with a low ceiling and neon lighting, and without a single window to relieve the sense of claustrophobia. The room was inhabited by four personages, or pieces of furniture. Their color was the same as the walls, their material wood, their form cubic. On each cube was another small cube with a latticed opening and below it a slot as in a mailbox. Carefully scrutinizing the grilled opening, you noted with alarm that from the interior you were being watched by something like eyes. The slots emitted, from time to time, a chorus of sighs or whisperings that the good Lord himself could not have made head or tail of. The placement of these cubes was such that they faced each other in the form of a square, composing a kind of conclave. I don't know how many minutes lapsed. At this point, the doctor came in and said to me, "My pardon, Bustos, for having kept you waiting. I was just out getting myself an advance ticket for today's match between the Palermo Juniors and the Spanish Sports." He went on, indicating the cubes, "Let me introduce you to Santiago Silberman, to retired clerk-of-court Ludueña, to Aquiles Molinari, and to Miss Bugard."

Out of the furniture came faint rumbling sounds. I quickly reached out a hand and, without the pleasure of shaking theirs, withdrew in good order, a frozen smile on my lips. Reaching the vestibule as best I could, I managed to stammer, "A drink. A stiff drink."

Narbondo came out of the lab with a graduated beaker filled with water and dissolved some effervescent drops into it. Blessed concoction—the wretched taste brought me to my senses. Then, the door to the small room closed and locked tight, came the explanation:

"I'm glad to see, my dear Bustos, that my immortals have made quite an impact on you. Whoever would have thought that *Homo sapiens,* Darwin's barely human ape, could achieve such perfection? This, my house, I assure you, is the only one in all Indo-America where Dr. Eric Stapledon's methodology has been fully applied. You recall, no doubt, the consternation that the death of the late lamented doctor, which took place in New Zealand, occasioned in scientific circles. I flatter myself, furthermore, for having implemented his precursory labors with a few Argentinean touches. In itself, the thesis—Newton's apple all over again—is fairly simple. The death of the body is a result, always, of the failure of some organ or other, call it the kidney, lungs, heart, or what you like. With the replacement of the organism's various components, in themselves perishable, with other corresponding stainless or polyethylene parts, there is no earthly reason whatever why the soul, why you yourself—Bustos Domecq—should not be immortal. None of your philosophical niceties here; the body can be vulcanized and from time to time recaulked, and so the mind keeps going. Surgery brings immortality to mankind. Life's essential aim has been attained—the mind lives on without fear of cessation. Each of our immortals is comforted by the certainty, backed by our firm's guarantee, of being a witness *in aeternum.* The brain, refreshed night and day by a system of electrical charges, is the last organic bulwark in which ball bearings and cells collaborate. The rest is Formica, steel, plastics. Respiration, alimentation, generation, mobility—elimination itself!—belong to the past. Our immortal is real estate. One or two minor touches are still missing, it's true. Oral articulation, dialogue, may still be improved. As for the costs, you need not worry yourself. By means of a procedure that circumvents legal red tape, the candidate transfers his property to us, and the Narbondo Company, Inc.—I, my son, his descendants—guarantees your upkeep, *in statu quo,* to the end of time. And, I might add, a money-back guarantee."

It was then that he laid a friendly hand on my

shoulder. I felt his will taking power over me. "Ha-ha! I see I've whetted your appetite, I've tempted you, dear Bustos. You'll need a couple of months or so to get your affairs in order and to have your stock portfolio signed over to us. As far as the operation goes, naturally, as a friend, I want to save you a little something. Instead of our usual fee of ten thousand dollars, for you, ninety-five hundred—in cash, of course. The rest is yours. It goes to pay your lodging, care, and service. The medical procedure in itself is painless. No more than a question of amputation and replacement. Nothing to worry about. On the eve, just keep yourself calm, untroubled. Avoid heavy meals, to-bacco, and alcohol, apart from your accustomed and imported, I hope, Scotch or two. Above all, refrain from impatience."

"Why two months?" I asked him. "One's enough, and then some. I come out of the anes-thesia and I'm one more of your cubes. You have my address and phone number. We'll keep in touch. I'll be back next Friday at the latest."

At the escape hatch he handed me the card of Nemirovski, Nemirovski, & Nemirovski, Counsel-ors-at-Law, who would put themselves at my dis-posal for all the details of drawing up the will. With perfect composure I walked to the subway entrance, then took the stairs at a run. I lost no time. That same night, without leaving the slight-est trace behind, I moved to the New Impartial, in whose register I figure under the assumed name of Aquiles Silberman. Here, in my bedroom at the far rear of this modest hotel, wearing a false beard and dark spectacles, I am setting down this ac-count of the facts.

Index Compiled
by H. Bustos Domecq